THE PRINCE CHARMING OF TEXAS

"How much farther is it?" Penny asked as she rode behind Dan on the steep, rocky, winding trail. After several hours in the saddle, they had to be getting close.

"Probably another two or three miles," he answered. "Are you doing all right?"

"Yes, though it's hard to believe that just a few weeks ago I was at the Chases' ball. It seems like an eternity—almost like another life."

She wondered what Richard and Amanda would think of her now if they saw her bundled up against the cold in workman's clothes, riding astride out in the middle of nowhere. She remembered how attentive Richard had been that night, and now it all seemed like a fairy tale.

Fairy tale—

She let her gaze linger on Dan, seeing the day's growth of beard on his jawline and liking how it added an aura of danger about him. She hadn't even realized how much she'd needed saving when he'd whisked her away from the ballroom. She hadn't realized how much she needed *him* . . .

RT BOOK REVIEWS PRAISES BOBBI SMITH, NEW YORK TIMES BESTSELLING AUTHOR!

RELENTLESS

"With its action-packed plot, colorful and accurate details, likable characters and multiple love stories, this is vintage Smith. It's exactly what [readers] adore from this consummate storyteller."

RUNAWAY

"In Smith's exciting Western, two wrongs do make a right. Continuous action, authentic dialogue and gripping tension ensnare the reader."

WANTED: THE HALF-BREED

"Smith fulfills her title of 'Queen of the Western Romance' in this fast-paced, suspenseful offering."

HIRED GUN

"Nobody does a Western better than Smith."

DEFIANT

"The talented Smith is in her element out West. This novel is fast-paced and filled with adventure and tender feelings . . . a very beautiful story."

HALFBREED WARRIOR

"Smith is the consummate storyteller. The pacing is quick, with snappy dialogue moving the story forward at breakneck speed."

BRAZEN

"As sexy and gritty as [Smith] has ever written."

HALF-MOON RANCH: HUNTER'S MOON

"Bobbi Smith is a terrific storyteller whose wonderful characters, good dialogue and compelling plot will keep you up all night."

LONE WARRIOR

"Fast paced, swift moving and filled with strong, well-crafted characters."

BOBBI SMITH

A Cowboy for Christmas

Dorchester
Publishing

DORCHESTER PUBLISHING

November 2010

Published by

Dorchester Publishing Co., Inc.
200 Madison Avenue
New York, NY 10016

ISBN 13: 978-1-4285-1159-0
E-ISBN: 978-1-4285-0898-9

The "DP" logo is the property of Dorchester Publishing Co., Inc.

Printed in the United States of America.

Visit us online at www.dorchesterpub.com.

This book is dedicated to all my readers—
Merry Christmas!

Also, thanks to the great librarians and historians who helped me with research:

Leslie and Debby at the St. Charles County Library

Adele Heagney and Richard Williams at the St. Louis Public Library

Jason Stratman at the Missouri Historical Society

Nick Ohlman at the Museum of Transportation

Author's Note—A Gift for You

Country-Western star Royal Wade Kimes (Royal WadeKimes.com) has written an original song especially for *A Cowboy for Christmas*! Check out "Penny, I Love You" at BobbiSmithBooks. com or DorchesterPub.com, where you can also get a free download of the song.

"Penny, I Love You" will also be featured on Royal's upcoming album.

A two-time winner of the Will Rogers award for best album and best video, Royal Wade Kimes has written songs for Garth Brooks, Diamond Rio, Gene Watson, and many others. He's been on the front cover of *True West* magazine and has been featured in *Country Weekly* and other magazines.

I hope you enjoy this hauntingly beautiful song based on my Christmas story. It's my special holiday gift to you.

Bobbi Smith

Prologue

St. Louis
Late 1850s

Twelve-year-old Danny Roland was cold and exhausted as he climbed into the back of the wagon with several of the other boys from the orphanage. Every morning except Sunday, one of the hands from the farm came to the orphans' home and picked up the older boys to take them out to the farm to work. They labored until almost sundown and then were returned to the asylum to eat dinner, sleep, and get ready to work again the following day.

Danny's mood was dark as he hung on to the side of the wagon to keep from getting thrown around on the rough ride back. Again, he wondered how he had ended up this way. Had it really only been six months ago that his mother had died from a terrible fever on their trip west and their father had abandoned him and his younger brother, Nick, there at the orphanage? The memory of that day still haunted him. He and Nick had begged their father to take them with him, but he'd refused. He had ridden away from the orphanage that afternoon, and they hadn't seen or heard from him since.

It seemed more like an eternity than just six months to Danny. At night, he would often lie in bed and pretend he was back home in Tennessee, safe with his mother and father, and that everything was fine, but his fantasy ended every morning just before dawn when the headmistress banged on the door to wake them up. Danny knew there was no escaping the truth anymore.

This was his life now.

This was his reality until he and Nick were adopted or until he was old enough to be released from the orphanage to care for himself.

Danny was determined to make the best of it, but for now he had to protect his brother. Nine-year-old Nick was having an even harder time than Dan was, for some of the mean boys had been picking on him. More than once, he'd had to defend his brother from their bullying. It was almost Christmas now, and Danny knew it was going to be a hard and painful time for him and his brother, since it would be their first Christmas without their mother and father. At least they still had each other.

When the wagon finally reached town and pulled to a stop in front of the orphanage, Danny felt a little better. He would soon be with Nick. He climbed down from the wagon and hurried inside where it was warm. He'd just come through the door when he was pulled aside by Miss Parker, one of the staff.

"The headmistress needs to see you. Give your coat to one of the other boys and come with me."

"Why does she want to see me?" Danny looked up at the elderly, white-haired woman in surprise. Only boys who were in trouble were taken to the office.

"I have no idea, young man. Let's go." Her tone was stern.

Danny took off his coat and handed it to Tommy, who stood back with the other boys watching warily as Miss Parker led him away. They knew it was serious when you were taken to see the headmistress.

"I wonder what he did," Tommy said.

"I don't know," another boy returned, "but I'm real glad I'm not Danny right now."

The rest of the boys hurried toward the room where they all slept so they could get cleaned up before it was time to say their evening prayers and then eat dinner.

Miss Helen looked up from her desk when the knock came at her office door. She'd heard the wagon pull up in front of the building and had been anxiously awaiting this moment. What she had to do next wasn't going to be easy, but there was no avoiding it.

"Come in," she called.

The door opened and Miss Parker brought in young Daniel Roland to stand before her desk.

"Thank you, Miss Parker." Miss Helen waited until the other woman had left and closed the door before continuing. "Daniel, I need to speak with you."

Her tone was icy, and he wondered what was wrong. He'd worked hard that day, so he was sure no one had complained about him. He watched her warily, not sure what to expect. "Yes, ma'am."

"I have some news for you."

A surge of hope shot through Danny. Maybe she'd gotten word from his father! Surely, since it was almost Christmas, he was finally coming back for them. It would be the perfect present to be living as a family again. His excitement grew as he waited for Miss Helen to begin.

"I'm not sure how you're going to handle it," she started.

The momentary happiness was replaced by a dark sense of dread.

"What is it?" he managed to choke out, fearing what was to come next.

"It's your brother."

"Nick?" Sudden panic filled Danny. "What about him? What's wrong? Was he hurt? Where is he?"

She hastened to reassure him. "No, your brother hasn't been injured. In fact, it's good news—for him. Today Nick was adopted by a wonderful family. He left this morning."

Nick was gone?

He'd been adopted?

Danny just stared at her. "I don't understand. Nick's *my* brother. He's *my family.*"

"Nick is with a new family now and just in time for the holidays." Miss Helen was tense as she awaited his reaction. The family who had adopted Nick couldn't afford to take both brothers, and they'd wanted a younger boy. She wasn't about to tell Danny about how his brother had been acting when they took him away. The sound of Nick's sobbing would stay with her for some time, but she knew in the long run that this was the chance for a better life for him.

"No!" Danny cried. He couldn't believe it. In a moment of pure desperation and panic, he ran from her office to find Nick. When he reached the boys' sleeping room, he found that the small chest where Nick had kept his few possessions, and it was then the reality of what had happened overwhelmed him. He sank down on the edge of the small bed and stared blindly down at the chest.

It was empty.

Now Danny had nothing, no one . . .

"Daniel—"

Danny looked up to find Miss Helen standing in the doorway.

"Who adopted him? I'm going after him!"

"No, you're not," she countered.

"Yes, I am! I'm going to bring him back! He should be here with me. I can take care of him."

He ran across the room, intent on finding out where his brother had been taken.

Miss Helen blocked the doorway, refusing to let him out into the hallway. "You're not going anywhere. You're staying right here."

"I can't stay here! I have to get Nick!" All the emotions he'd been trying to control overwhelmed him.

"The Miller family isn't from the area. They left town this morning." She didn't give him any more information than that. She knew how headstrong Danny could be, and she didn't want him to think he could go find his brother and bring him back. "Maybe when Nick is older he'll get in touch with you, but for now, you're staying here—and that's final."

Danny was filled with rage. "No!"

He tried to run past her, wanting to race from the orphanage and search for Nick.

Miss Helen had known this wouldn't be easy. Being separated from his brother so suddenly after already having lost his mother and father had to be traumatic for him, but she would not tolerate any trouble from him. Danny was known for being stubborn and occasionally defiant. She ruled with an iron hand, and the boys who didn't obey her suffered the consequences. She grabbed him by the arm to stop him. "Did you hear me, young man? I said you will be staying here and behaving yourself."

Danny struggled to break away, but her hold was too strong.

"I think you need a little time in 'the cell' to calm down," she declared. She hauled him out into the hall and down to the small, dark, windowless room that was hardly bigger than a closet. She unlocked the door and put him inside.

"If you behave yourself, I may let you out at bedtime."

With that, she turned and stalked out, locking the door behind her.

Danny leaned back against the wall and sank down to the floor. Only after he heard her move off did he finally give in to his heartbreak and begin to cry.

He was alone now.

Really alone.

Nick was gone.

Danny didn't know why this had happened to him. He tried to pray, but suddenly found himself wondering if there was any point. He'd lost everything—his mother, his father, and now his brother. He didn't understand why God had let this happen.

It was some time later when Danny finally managed to pull himself together. In anger and disgust, he wiped away his tears and faced his future. There was no going back. The past was just that—it was past—it was over.

In that moment, Danny realized he had no

choice. He had to grow up now and become a man. It wasn't going to be easy, but nothing in his life had been easy since his mother's death, and he couldn't see how anything would get better in the future.

A fierce resolution filled Danny. He had promised Nick he would protect him and keep him safe when their father had abandoned them, and he meant to do just that. Somehow, he was going to find his brother. He had made a promise to him and he was going to keep it.

It was after dinner when Miss Parker came to let him out of the closet. She had not brought him any food, and he didn't say a word. He just returned to the sleeping room. The other boys watched him with open curiosity, but he didn't speak to them. He got cleaned up and changed into his pajamas and went to bed, pulling the covers up high.

Miss Parker came to check on them and then put out the lamp so they would go to sleep. Once she was sure they were all bedded down and quiet, she left the room and closed the door behind her.

"Danny . . ."

Danny heard the whisper and recognized that it was Tommy. "Go away."

"No, Danny, here." The young boy poked him in the shoulder.

Irritated, Danny threw his covers off and rolled over, ready for trouble, only to discover the young boy had somehow managed to sneak a piece of bread out of the dining room.

"I brought it for you." Tommy held the bread out to him. "I thought you might be hungry after working all day and not getting any dinner." He liked Danny and had looked up to him for the way he took care of his brother. He'd always wished he had a big brother just like him.

"Thanks." Danny was truly touched by his unexpected act of kindness. If Tommy had gotten caught sneaking food out of the dining room, he would have been punished. Danny took the offered bread and began to eat it.

"I'm gonna miss Nick," Tommy said. "I can't believe he's gone."

Danny knew Nick and Tommy had played together whenever they could. "Neither can I," he told him.

They looked at each other in silence for a moment and then Tommy went on to bed, knowing he'd get in trouble if anyone caught him up and moving around.

Danny finished eating the bread and then lay back down. He pretended to be sleeping, but, in truth, he was waiting until he was sure everyone was asleep. Only then did he risk making his escape. With great stealth, he gathered his few belongings. He took the pillowcase off his pillow and used it to stow his things. Very quietly he climbed out the window and dropped to the alleyway below.

He couldn't stay at the orphanage.

Not anymore.

He wasn't sure how he was going to do it, but he was going after his brother, and once he'd found him, they would leave this town and never come back.

Filled with resolve, Danny moved off into the night to begin his search.

The following morning, the boys were shocked when they woke up to find Danny gone. When Miss Helen learned that he'd disappeared, she immediately sent some of the adults out to try to find him, but Tommy and the other orphans had a feeling they would never see Danny again.

It was one week later, on Christmas Eve, when Tommy was awakened by the sound of a pebble hitting the window to the bedroom there in the orphanage. Excitement filled him for a moment, for he believed he might be hearing Santa and his reindeer, but then another pebble hit the window and he knew it wasn't Santa coming to the orphanage.

Tommy crept from his bed to push the curtain aside and look out into the dark alley. Since he knew it wasn't Santa, he hoped it would be Danny coming back. He'd missed the older boy.

"Tommy!" came Nick's hushed call when his friend appeared in the window.

"Nick?" He recognized Nick's voice and was shocked to see him hiding in the alley.

"Get Danny for me!"

"Danny? I can't!"

"Why not?" Nick came out of his hiding place and moved closer. He wanted so much to see his brother. He needed to be with Danny.

"Danny's not here!" Tommy called back.

Their conversation woke some of the other boys, who came to join Tommy at the window. "What's going on?" one asked.

"It's Nick. He's back, looking for Danny," he told them quietly.

"What do you mean Danny's not here?" Nick was shocked by the news. "Did he get adopted, too?"

"Wait there," Tommy told him, and he started to sneak out of the sleeping room.

"What are you doing?" one of the older boys asked, knowing he would get in trouble.

"I gotta go talk to Nick. I gotta tell him what happened."

With that, Tommy left the room, and after putting on his coat, he moved silently down the hall to slip out the back door. He found Nick waiting for him and saw several of the other boys hanging out the window watching them.

"Why did you come back?" Tommy asked. "You got adopted."

Nick looked miserable. "I ran away. I had to. The Millers were nice enough, but Danny's my family, and he always will be. It's Christmas—I want to be with my brother. Where is he?"

"When Danny found out you were gone, he ran away. He snuck off that first night after you were adopted, and we haven't seen him since. I'm sure he was going after you. Miss Helen even had some people searching the streets for him, but they never found him. Nobody knows where he went."

Nick stared at his friend in complete misery. The home he'd been taken to was a good one. The couple who'd adopted him were kind, God-fearing people who'd treated him well, but he needed his brother. He was lost without Danny. He didn't know what to do now. It had taken him three days to make it back to the orphanage. And now to find Danny gone . . .

"What is going on out here?" Miss Helen demanded as she came out of the building with several of the older boys who'd gone to get her.

Nick and Tommy were scared, but they knew better than to try to run away.

Nick spoke up. "It's my fault." With shoulders slumped, he went to face the headmistress. "Tommy didn't do anything, Miss Helen. It's me, Nick."

"Nick?" She was shocked to find the young boy standing there before her in the middle of the night. "What are you doing here? You should be with the Millers."

"I ran away."

"But your family . . ." She could only imagine

what his adoptive parents were going through right then, worrying about him.

"Danny is my family, Miss Helen."

Miss Helen ordered Tommy and all the other boys to go back inside to bed. Then she took Nick to her office and forced him to sit in the chair before her desk. This was Christmas Eve. Things were supposed to be quiet and peaceful, and now she had to deal with this.

"What do you think you're doing, running away like this?"

"I can't go back to the Millers without my brother." Nick knew she was furious, but right then he didn't care. Nothing mattered but being with Danny.

"You have to," she said. "As I'm sure Tommy told you, Danny is gone. He ran away the same day you left for your new home."

"Where did he go?" He looked up at her in agony, worrying about his brother. "Didn't he leave a note or something?"

"No. We have no idea where he disappeared to. We looked for him for several days, but found no trace of him."

"Danny's got to be here somewhere." All he could think about was his poor brother alone, hungry, and cold on the dark, scary city streets.

"He's gone, Nick, and I don't believe he's coming back."

"He's probably still out there looking for me."

"Whatever the case, I need to return you to your new parents. I'm sure they're worried sick about you. They love you so much. Why, they're probably on their way back here, looking for you right now."

Nick wanted to just get up right then and run away from the orphanage. He wanted to take off and search for his brother, but there was little hope that he would ever find Danny on his own, not after so many days had already passed. A great and heavy sorrow filled his heart, but he knew he couldn't give up. To satisfy Miss Helen, he answered, "Yes, ma'am."

Miss Helen was glad he hadn't tried to cause any more trouble. She couldn't wait for morning to get there, so she could take the necessary steps to reunite him with his adoptive family. At least, the Millers would have a blessed Christmas, getting Nick back.

Chapter One

Sagebrush, Texas
Eleven years later

Hank Moran was filled with rage as he sat at a back table in the Gold Dust Saloon, drinking heavily. The day before, Jack Anderson had fired him from his job as foreman on the Lazy Ace. He'd known Jack had a reputation as being a hard man to work for when he hired on, but he never thought Jack would turn out to be as bad as he was. Hank had hated the time he'd spent working for him and now that he'd been fired, he hated the rancher even more. Humiliated, he kept drinking and planned just how he was going to get even.

Sally had been waiting on Hank since he'd come in several hours earlier. She'd heard the talk about him losing his job and had recognized immediately that he was in one ugly mood. She'd made it a point to stay away from him except to serve his whiskey, for she knew from experience Hank would look for a fight when he got this drunk.

As Sally made her way toward Hank's table to get him a refill of whiskey, she noticed the good-looking stranger who'd just walked into the saloon.

Tall and darkly handsome, the new man stood out in a room crowded with drunken, rowdy, unwashed ranch hands. She offered him a quick smile but kept moving. She'd definitely find the time to see what he wanted as soon as she could, but right then she had to get Hank's drink to him before he started trouble.

"Here you go, Hank."

"'Bout time you got here," he snapped.

"Wanted to make sure it was just perfect for you," she purred, trying not to sound irritated as she set the tumbler of whiskey before him. "You look like you could use some fun, Hank."

"There's only one thing I want to do," Hank snarled.

"What's that?" she asked, believing he was going to say he wanted to get bedded that night.

Hank looked up at her. "I want to get even with Jack Anderson for what he did to me."

His expression was so full of hate, Sally found herself feeling very uneasy around him. "Well, for right now, drink up, and enjoy yourself."

She moved away, hoping to get a chance to flirt with the new fella, who was making his way up to the bar.

Dan had taken a quick look around the saloon and then gone to the bar to order a shot of whiskey.

"You're new in town, aren't you?" the bartender asked as he set the tumbler on the bar and filled it with a generous amount of liquor.

"Just rode in this afternoon. Nice town you've

got here. Seems real peaceful," Dan said, pushing the money for the drink across the bar to him.

"You want trouble, just show up on payday weekends. Things can get a little wild then, but you're right—for the most part it's pretty quiet here in Sagebrush, and we like it that way."

"That's good to hear," Dan said, and he meant it. In the years he'd been on his own, he'd moved around a lot. He'd been in some real bad places and he'd met some real bad people. He'd been through hard times, but he'd managed to survive by working hard, learning how to use a gun, and watching his own back. He knew no one else was going to do that for him. He had to take care of himself.

"You need anything else, just yell. My name's Wayne."

Dan just nodded to him as he lifted his glass to take a drink. He was ready to settle in and relax for a while.

"You got everything you need, handsome?" asked a saloon girl as she sashayed up next to him. She leaned back against the bar to give him a full view of the low-cut bodice of her dress and smiled brightly.

"Now that you're here, I do." He returned her smile. "Can I buy you a drink?"

"I'd like that a lot."

Dan signaled Wayne, and the bartender moved back down to the end of the bar to see what he wanted.

"Give the lady whatever she wants," Dan said, paying him.

"I do like the way you think." She gave him a look full of promise.

Wayne poured the drink and was about to move away to take care of his other customers when Jack Anderson walked into the saloon. The hair on the back of Wayne's neck rose. Considering the mood Hank was in, this was trouble. He just hoped the former foreman stayed so busy drinking that he wouldn't notice Jack at the bar. Wayne wanted to avoid any kind of fight between the two men tonight.

"Evening, Jack," Wayne said, keeping his voice down. He set about pouring the rancher a glass of his favorite bourbon. He wanted to ask how everything was going out at the Lazy Ace, but hesitated. "What brings you to town tonight?"

"I had a few things I had to—"

"Anderson?"

Hank's shout brought a sudden silence to the room.

Jack hadn't noticed Hank when he'd come in, but it didn't surprise him to hear the man's slurred yell from the back of the room. Hank had proven himself to be nothing but a drunken troublemaker right from the start, and Jack was glad he'd finally gotten rid of him. Jack kept his drink in his hand as he slowly turned to look in Hank's direction.

"Yes, Hank?" Jack said calmly. He didn't want

any trouble with the fool. He just wanted him to move on.

Hank was as drunk as he'd ever been, and his fury was real as he stood, knocking his chair over in the effort. He staggered toward the bar, ready for a fight.

One of the other men sitting at a nearby table knew what was going to happen, and he got up, hoping to stop Hank from doing anything too stupid. He grabbed Hank's arm, but Hank hit him savagely, and the man fell heavily to the floor.

Hank gave the other men standing around a threatening look. "Get away from me! All of you!"

Dan had dealt with men like this one before, and he knew what was coming. He moved away from the bar and drew the young barmaid with him.

"Get out of sight," Dan told her in a low voice as others in the room scrambled to avoid getting caught up in the coming confrontation.

"Hank's out for revenge," she whispered frantically. "Jack just threw him off his ranch."

Dan nodded to her and turned back to watch the two men as they faced each other down.

Jack's expression was one of disgust as he set his drink aside. He slowly looked at the drunken fool who'd come to stand before him. "It's over and done with, Hank. Let it go."

"No, it's not over and done with," Hank threatened.

"Yes," Jack inisisted, "it is."

He started to turn his back. He hoped ignoring him would make him go away, but it didn't work.

Jack's actions only enraged Hank even more. Hank drew his gun and held it straight at the other man. "You're wrong, Jack!"

"Hank, put the gun away," Wayne ordered from behind the bar, more than a little tense. He never thought Hank would be stupid enough to draw his gun.

As a bartender, he'd seen this many times— stupid men doing stupid things when they were trying to prove they weren't stupid. Wayne knew Hank didn't realize he was only showing everyone just how right Jack had been to fire him. Wayne edged toward the end of the bar where he kept his shotgun.

"Don't even think about going for your shotgun, Wayne," Hank raged, glaring around the room. "And the rest of you, stay out of this! This is between the boss and me." He looked back to Jack and motioned toward the door. "Move, Jack. Go on, get outside."

"There's nothing to be gained from this," Wayne warned him. Instead of stepping up to help, his other patrons were backing off. They knew how dangerous Hank was when he got this drunk. Wayne could only hope someone had managed to sneak out the back without Hank seeing him and go for the sheriff.

Dan knew the drunken fool had murder on his mind. He glanced around the saloon and realized no one else was going to do anything to help. He was going to have to stop the drunk by himself. Dan waited just long enough for Anderson to reach the swinging doors before making his move.

"Anderson, run!" Dan shouted as he charged forward and launched himself at Hank.

Hank panicked and got off one wild shot in Jack's direction just as Dan tackled him from his blind side. They crashed to the floor in a violent struggle, rolling savagely around until Dan was able to knock the gun out of Hank's hand.

In all his years on his own, Dan had become pretty good at fighting. He finally managed to overpower Hank and knock him unconscious. Grabbing up the gun, Dan got to his feet and stood over him. He watched Hank for a moment, wanting to make sure he wasn't going to cause any more trouble.

Wayne rushed to his side, armed with his shotgun, ready to help.

"That was real brave of you," he told the stranger, impressed by his quick action. He had little doubt the man had saved Jack's life, and then, thinking of Jack, he yelled, "Jack! You all right?"

Jack came back in through the swinging doors, holding his bloodied upper arm. "He winged me, but it's not bad." Jack turned to the newcomer, his expression serious. "I owe you my life."

"I was glad to help," Dan offered, relieved the older man hadn't been more seriously wounded.

"What's your name?" Jack asked.

"Dan Roland."

"Well, Dan Roland, I'm Jack Anderson, and I want to buy you a drink." Jack looked to Wayne.

The crowd in the saloon had moved in closer to see what had happened now that all the fighting and shooting were over.

"Harry! Charley! Get Hank over to Sheriff Thompson at the jail. Now!" Wayne yelled to two of his regulars. "Tell him what happened and make sure he locks Hank up."

The two men grabbed the unconscious man and hauled him away.

"Carl, go get the doc," Wayne instructed another man sitting at the far end of the bar. "Jack needs his arm looked after."

Carl hurried to do as the barkeep had ordered.

"Jack, let's tie that arm up with this towel, till Doc Clemens gets here." Wayne hurried back behind the bar to put his shotgun away and get one of the bar towels. He went back to Jack and quickly helped bind his upper arm to stop the blood flow. That done, he got his bottle of bourbon and refilled Jack's glass. "I'm thinking you could use a stiff one right now. Drink up—on the house."

"Thanks, Wayne," Jack said. "Give my new friend Dan Roland here whatever he wants. I'm buying his."

Wayne looked to Dan. "Want some of my bourbon?"

"That'll be fine," Dan told him.

"Looks like we were both wrong, thinking it was a peaceful night in Sagebrush," the barkeep said as he quickly served him his drink and re-filled Jack's glass again.

Dan couldn't help smiling. "I was going to say, if this was peaceful, I can imagine what your payday weekends are like."

Wayne chuckled as he moved away.

"Let's go sit down," Jack invited, taking up his glass and leading the way over to a table.

Calm returned to the saloon.

"Do you always jump into fights that aren't your own?" Jack asked as they sat down again.

Dan took a drink of his liquor and gave him a half smile. "Only if I think somebody could use my help."

"That can get you into trouble sometimes," Jack joked.

"I know. It already has," Dan returned.

"What brought you to Sagebrush? Are you passing through or planning on staying around for a while?"

"I was just passing through when I rode in."

"You need work?"

"You hiring?"

Jack looked him straight in the eye as he answered, "You got any ranching experience?"

"I do."

"The foreman's job is open at the Lazy Ace. Are you interested?"

"I am."

They were about to say more when Doc Clemens hurried into the saloon carrying his black bag. He stopped just inside the doors. "What's this I hear? Did Jack get shot?"

"He's over at the table in back, Doc," Wayne directed.

"Well, he can't be hurting too bad if he's still sitting here drinking," he remarked with a grin when he spotted Jack downing his drink at the table across the room. He went over to treat his wound. "Got yourself in more trouble, did you, Jack?"

"Don't I always, Doc?" He and the doctor had known each other for years and were good friends.

The doctor put his bag on the table and quickly untied the towel. He tore away what was left of his shirtsleeve and set about examining his arm.

"You were one real lucky man, Jack," Doc Clemens said as he set about cleaning the wound. "It just grazed you. You're going to be sore for a time, but it isn't serious."

Jack grimaced a little as the doctor poured alcohol on the wound. He took another drink of his bourbon and locked his jaw against the pain as he waited for him to finish.

"There." The doctor finished wrapping the wound in a clean bandage. "That should do you."

"Thanks, Doc," Jack said as he paid him.

"You're welcome. I'm just glad it wasn't anything worse. You stay out of trouble, Jack."

"I'm trying," he told him with a half laugh.

"Just keep drinking your bourbon for the pain."

"I like your kind of doctoring."

"I thought you would. What's going to happen to Hank? He isn't going to get out of jail and come after you again, is he?"

Wayne spoke up from behind the bar. "No, I'm sure the sheriff will keep him locked up. We got a lot of witnesses who heard Hank threaten Jack and saw him take the shot at him. He won't get off easy on this one."

"Can I buy you a drink, Doc?" Jack offered.

"I appreciate the offer, but I need to get back to the office. If it gives you any real trouble, just let me know."

"I will."

Jack looked over at Dan again once the doctor had gone. "So, did I just hire myself a new foreman?"

"Yes, sir. You did," Dan answered, meeting his gaze straight on.

"Welcome to the Lazy Ace."

Chapter Two

Three years later
The Lazy Ace

After a few days away working stock, Dan was real glad to be back at the ranch to get a hot meal and sleep in a clean, warm bed. He dismounted and was starting to unsaddle his horse when Fred, the bunkhouse cook, came out to speak with him.

"It's good you're here," Fred began.

Dan immediately noticed how serious the older man was and grew worried. "Is something wrong?"

Fred's expression was troubled as he answered, "Oh yeah."

"What is it?"

"It's Jack." He glanced up toward the main house. "The doc was here yesterday and . . ."

Dan knew it had to be serious if Jack had agreed to see the doctor. Over the years he'd worked for him, Dan had come to understand what a strong-willed, hard-driven man Jack Anderson was. Jack didn't back down when he believed he was right, and he always tried to tough things out when times got bad. "What happened?"

"Don't know for sure. It came on real sud-denlike and after he finally agreed to let me get the doc to come see him . . ." Fred paused as he glanced up toward the main house. "The news was bad."

"How bad?"

Fred looked up at Dan and told him the grim truth. "The doc says he ain't got long to live."

Dan heard him, but he didn't want to believe it. As strong and vital a man as Jack was, it seemed impossible he could be this ill. "Why?"

"Something with his heart, I think."

"Can't Doc Clemens do something for him?"

"The doc said it was just a matter of time, a few months if Jack's lucky."

"I've got to see him," Dan said. Jack was the closest thing he had to a family. The thought that he was sick and might be dying tormented him. He had to do everything in his power to help Jack through this.

"I'll finish tending to your horse for you," Fred offered.

"Thanks."

Dan hurried up to the house and found Jack sitting at the desk in his office.

"You're back," Jack said, looking up as Dan entered the room. "How did things go?"

"Fine until now."

Jack saw how serious his expression was. "I take it you've already talked to Fred."

Dan nodded as he came to stand before him.

He immediately noticed how pale Jack was. Generally, he was a hardy, robust man, but there was little color in his face now. His features seemed drawn and almost haggard, as if the life was somehow draining out of him. Dan found it hard to believe that he could have gotten this weak in just the short time he'd been gone. "He saw me ride in and came out to tell me the news."

"It's not good," Jack said without emotion, having already accepted his fate. He'd known even before he'd seen the doctor that he was feeling worse than he ever had, and the news the doc had given him hadn't surprised him.

"Maybe the doc's wrong." Dan wanted to encourage him to fight whatever was ailing him.

"No, he's not wrong," Jack told him, looking up at him to meet his gaze.

In that moment, Dan could see the pain mirrored in his friend's eyes and realized just how much Jack was suffering. "There's got to be something we can do."

In the time he'd spent alone since Doc Clemens had given him the bad news, Jack had done a lot of thinking. He had accomplished a lot in his life, building the Lazy Ace into a successful ranch, but there was one thing more he had to take care of before he died. He would never be able to rest in peace unless he got Penny to come home.

"Yes, there is. I need your help."

Dan had no idea what Jack was about to ask, but he could deny his friend nothing.

"I need you to go back to St. Louis and bring my daughter home. I need to see Penny again before I die."

"Your daughter?"

Jack had rarely spoken of his wife and daughter. What little Dan knew was that Jack's wife had left him six years ago and had taken their daughter with her. The other hands had told him how Jack had made a trip back to St. Louis to see them some months after they'd left, but his wife had been so determined not to have anything more to do with him that he'd stayed away ever since. Jack had tried to bring Penny back to the ranch for visits, but his wife had refused all his efforts, and the hands knew he'd hardly ever heard from his daughter. When Jack had gotten the news of his wife's death two years before, he'd tried to contact Penny again hoping she would come home then, but when she had not responded to his letters, he'd given up. Despite all that, Dan knew this time things were different.

Jack handed him a small oil portrait of Penny he kept on his desk. "Yes. Go get her for me, Dan." He opened the top drawer and took out a sealed envelope. "I know she might refuse to come, but give her this letter."

"I will," he promised. He took the letter.

"Here's the money you'll need for the trip." Jack took another envelope out of the drawer and gave it to him.

"Why don't you come with me?"

"No, I need to stay here on the Lazy Ace. Bring her home, Dan. If I could just have her here for Christmas . . ." He fell quiet for a moment, remembering how they'd celebrated the holidays when she was young and living on the ranch.

"All right."

Dan realized it probably wasn't going to be an easy task to convince her to give up city living and return to Texas. If she'd had little to no contact with her father in all this time, he wondered if she would even care that Jack was sick and dying. Somehow, he was going to have to find a way to convince her to return to the ranch. Friend that Jack was to him, Dan knew he wouldn't return without her.

"I can get ready and head into town tonight. There should be a stage coming through tomorrow."

"Thank you."

Taking the envelopes with him, Dan started from the room without saying any more.

"Dan—"

Jack's call stopped Dan before he could walk out the door. He turned back to see his friend looking very weak and frail.

"Hurry back."

"I'll get her back to you as fast as I can," Dan promised, and he meant it. One way or another, he was going to see Jack reunited with his daughter. It was the least he could do for a man who'd given him so much. He left the main house and went to pack.

As foreman, he had a small two-room house off to the side of the bunkhouse. Some of the hands were wondering what he was doing when they saw him come out carrying a traveling bag. Dan quickly explained the reason for his trip.

"Jack's going to need you boys more than ever now. Lou, you take over running things while I'm gone, and all of you keep a close eye on Jack," he instructed.

"We will," Lou said, giving Dan a reassuring pat on the shoulder.

"I'll get back here with Penny as fast as I can."

"Good luck to you," Lou said.

"Thanks. I think I may need it."

"That you might," he agreed. "As a little girl, Penny was as headstrong as her father. I can just imagine what kind of woman she's grown into after living in the city all this time."

Fred put in, "I wonder why Jack even wants to see her again. She hasn't been back in all these years."

"The ranch will be hers when he dies," Lou pointed out, "so she'd better come back and show her father some respect." He looked to Dan. "I'll ride with you into town and bring your horse back. You're going to be gone a spell."

"I know." Dan was grim. "There's no fast way to do this, but if I can get out of Sagebrush tomorrow, hopefully I can have her back here before

Christmas. I have to bring her home before anything happens to Jack."

Lou could tell Dan was determined not to fail. "If anyone can bring Penny back in time, it'll be you. You've never let Jack down yet, and you won't this time, either. Come on, let's get you into town."

Fifteen days later

Penny was excited as she pulled another gown out of her wardrobe to show her friend. "Since you don't like the pink dress, what about this one, Amanda?"

Amanda smiled as Penny held up the turquoise dress. "That's definitely the one! Try it on and let me see."

"All right, but you'll have to help."

Penny presented her back to her friend and waited while Amanda unfastened the buttons. That done, Penny quickly took it off and slipped into the modestly cut, turquoise gown before turning around to pose.

"Well, what do you think?

Amanda nodded in delight. "I was right. It's perfect! Richard will be so impressed."

"Good. I do want to look my best tonight."

"You will," Amanda said. "Everybody who's anybody will be there." She paused. "Penny . . ."

Amanda's tone was so serious all of a sudden that Penny glanced over at her questioningly. "What?"

"Do you love him?"

Penny was quiet for a moment as she thought of the handsome, debonair Richard Williams. "I really haven't gotten to know him that well yet," she answered.

"How could you not love him? He's handsome and he's rich! What more does a man need to win your heart?"

"It sounds to me like you're in love with him!" she countered, laughing.

"It would be unrequited." Amanda sighed dramatically.

"I like Richard. He's always been a gentleman with me, and I will admit he is good-looking."

"Very," she agreed, thinking how the tall, blond banker set female hearts fluttering all over town—her own especially.

"I'm just not ready to think about marrying anyone yet, no matter what Aunt Matilda says. After what happened between my mother and my father, I don't know if I'll ever get married."

"Penny!" She was shocked by her friend's honesty. "You were definitely not meant to be an old maid!"

"And what's wrong with being an old maid?" Penny grinned at her impishly. "I think it would be rather liberating to be free to do whatever you wanted to do, whenever you wanted to do it."

Amanda couldn't help laughing. "I've always known you were a wild one. Society doesn't respect a woman without a suitable husband."

Penny gave her a mischievous look. "Do we really care what society thinks?"

"Well, I know that society thinks we should show up on time at the ball tonight. I'd better go get ready myself. I'll see you later."

"Yes, you will," Penny said as her friend left the room.

Amanda stopped by the parlor on her way out. "It was lovely to see you again, Aunt Matilda."

The older woman smiled, glad that Penny's friend liked her enough to call her aunt, too. "You as well," she returned. "You and your parents will be at the Chases' ball tonight, won't you?"

"Of course! We wouldn't miss it for the world. I can't wait! Penny is going to look so pretty. She's picked the turquoise gown to wear."

"Good, good. I'm sure you'll both be lovely."

Matilda walked Amanda to the door. She believed the young woman was a good influence on her niece, and she was quite fond of her.

When Amanda had gone, Matilda started upstairs to speak to Penny. Having never married and had children of her own, she had accepted her sister Elizabeth and her niece into her home when they'd returned from Texas. They had lived comfortably together on the family money they had inherited. But since Elizabeth's death, life had become more complicated. She could only hope she was doing all she could do to help her niece.

Matilda knew Elizabeth would be proud of the lady her daughter had become. Penny was strikingly beautiful with her dark hair and eyes and slender figure, and there was no doubt she was a very intelligent young woman. She just hoped Penny married well when the time came and that her marriage would be a happy one—unlike her mother's.

Elizabeth had become so estranged from her husband that she destroyed any attempt at communication between him and his daughter. Matilda still felt guilty for not telling her niece that her father had written, but she'd promised her sister to keep silent.

Matilda reached Penny's room and knocked on the door. "May I come in?"

"Of course," Penny responded.

Matilda let herself in to find her niece had changed back into her day gown. "Amanda said you've chosen the turquoise gown for tonight."

"Yes, will you help me pick out what jewelry to wear with it?"

The older woman was delighted to have been asked. They went through her jewelry box searching for the perfect necklace, finally selecting a strand of pearls and matching earrings.

"These will be perfect with it," Matilda told her. "And we'll need to leave by seven."

"I'll be ready," Penny promised.

"Good. Now it's my turn. I'd better go pick out

which gown I'm going to wear. I certainly want to make myself presentable. This is an important evening."

"You'll be pretty in whatever you decide on."

"I do love having you around, dear." Matilda was smiling as she left her niece's bedroom.

When her aunt had gone, Penny sat down on her bed, her thoughts all on the evening to come. It would be nice to see Richard at the Chases' Thanksgiving ball tonight. As Amanda had said, he was good-looking, and she did enjoy his company. He certainly was one of the best dancers in town, that was for sure. It was just when Amanda had asked her if she was in love with him that she'd grown troubled. After watching what had happened to her parents, she wasn't sure she could ever risk falling in love and get married.

Facing the truth of her feelings wasn't easy for Penny, so she quickly put those thoughts from her. She had a party to think about. For now, she was going to concentrate on just having fun that evening.

Chapter Three

Dan was glad he'd brought his heavy coat along as he stood outside the train station in the cold weather. He couldn't help noticing how much the city had changed in the years he'd been away. The station was a busy place, and the streets were crowded with warmly dressed folks coming and going. He was impressed. St. Louis was called "the Gateway to the West" and he knew it was true. He'd certainly headed west when he'd left.

Dan hired a carriage and told the driver the address for the orphanage. He wanted to see it before he checked in at the hotel.

The driver gave him a puzzled look as he helped him with his bags. "You sure you want to go there?"

"I'm sure," Dan answered.

"All right," the driver agreed as they started off, "but there ain't much left there to see."

"Why? What happened?"

"The orphans' home burned down some years back and nobody ever bothered to rebuild it."

"What about the children?"

"There are other homes in the city. They took them in." He asked, "Why do you care?"

"I lived at the orphanage for a while."

"Oh."

The driver fell silent, knowing by the man's tone that he didn't want to talk about it anymore. He drove on to the address and then he stopped the carriage to give him a chance to look around.

Dan recognized the neighborhood and found himself just staring at the lot where the building had been. He didn't bother to get down and walk around. He knew the driver had been right. There wasn't anything left—only an empty lot.

Empty—

Dan realized that certainly fit, for that was what his life had been after he'd lost his brother.

"All right, take me on to the Planter's House Hotel," Dan directed, putting the past behind him, he believed, once and for all.

He'd wasted enough time on memories.

Now it was time to take care of Jack's business.

It was late in the afternoon when Dan finally settled into his hotel room. He was tired, but he would worry about getting some rest later. What mattered now was finding Jack's daughter and convincing her to return to Texas with him. He'd checked the railroad departure times before he'd left the station and knew that one was scheduled to leave the following afternoon. If things worked out as he hoped they would, he could have Penny on that train and be heading back to the ranch the very next day. He had to get Penny back to Texas and her father as quickly as he could.

Dan ordered a bath brought up to his room. When the tub of steaming water was delivered, he quickly got cleaned up, shaved, and donned his last set of clean clothes. He put on his coat and his Stetson and glanced down at his gun belt lying on the bed. He thought seriously about strapping it on, but finally decided against it. Unarmed, he left the room to get directions from the clerk at the front desk.

"You'll need a driver to take you," the clerk advised, after telling him how to get to the address he'd given him. "There should be a carriage just outside."

"Thanks."

Dan was impressed by Matilda Hathaway's home as the carriage drew to a stop out in front. A three-story brick mansion with a wide front porch, it spoke of wealth and luxury, and he grimaced inwardly at the thought of trying to convince Jack's daughter to give all this up and return to the ranch. He had no doubt after all her years of living this way that she was a spoiled, arrogant city girl now, who probably didn't care at all about her father or the ranch.

"Wait for me," Dan told the driver. He hoped Penny was home and would be willing to meet with him, but there was no way to know for sure.

"Yes, sir," the driver answered.

Dan made his way through the wrought-iron gate and up the walkway to the porch. He knocked on the door and stood back as he waited for someone to answer it. He wasn't surprised to find a maid opening the door.

"May I help you?" she asked, more than a little surprised and intimidated to find a tall, broad-shouldered man who looked to be a cowboy standing there before her.

"My name's Dan Roland. I work for Jack Anderson, and I'm here to see Penny Anderson," he answered.

"I'm sorry, Miss Anderson isn't at home right now. You'll have to come back tomorrow." She started to close the door on the stranger and was shocked when he blocked the door and stepped inside, into the front hall. He was such a powerful figure that she took several steps back away from him, feeling threatened. "Sir, really, you mustn't force your way in—"

"I'm not forcing my way in. I just need you to answer a question for me," Dan said.

She wasn't quite sure what to think of him, but he had said he worked for Penny's father, so that explained the edge of danger about him. She had heard all the tales from Penny's mother when she'd first returned to live with Miss Matilda, about what life was really like out West, and she'd fully understood why she'd wanted to return to live in the city. "What is it you want to know?" she asked.

"If Miss Anderson isn't here, where is she? It's important I speak with her tonight. I have a message for her from her father, and I need to deliver it to her as soon as possible," he explained quickly. He didn't want the woman to feel threatened by his presence, but he wasn't going to sit around and wait until the following day to let Penny know what was going on.

"If you'd like to tell me what it is, I can give her the message when she comes home, but it will be much later tonight."

"No, I need to speak with her myself."

"Oh—" For this young man to have made the trip all the way from Texas, she knew whatever he had to tell her was important. He was a stranger, but the women would be safe within a home full of friends. "Penny and her aunt are attending a private ball at the Chase home on Lucas Place." Sadie gave him the address. "You'll find them there."

"I thank you for your help, ma'am," Dan said as he turned and started back down the walk.

Sadie watched him go, wondering what the message was. She certainly hoped it was good news and not bad, but she had her doubts, as serious as the young man had been.

Sadie wondered, too, what the fashionable Chase family was going to think when a cowboy showed up at their front door. Dan Roland would certainly give the older ladies something to talk about. She was sure of that.

Dan climbed back in the carriage and gave the driver the new address, then sat back to wait out the ride. He was even more tense now as they made their way through the city streets toward the Chase home. It was going to be even more difficult interrupting a social event to find her, but he had no choice.

Dan hoped Jack's health was holding up. Even with the best of luck, it would probably be several more weeks before he could get Penny back home.

As the carriage stopped in front of the Chase mansion, it was obvious there was a large party going on. The mansion was brightly lit, and music could be heard coming from inside.

"I'll be back as fast as I can," Dan said.

"I'll be waiting."

Dan went up to the house and knocked on the door.

The servant who answered knew right away that the man standing before him was not one of the invited guests. "Yes, sir. How may I help you?" His tone was haughty and unwelcoming.

"I'm here to see Miss Penny Anderson," Dan answered.

"May I see you invitation, please?"

"I don't have an invitation. I—"

"I'm sorry, you'll have to leave, then. This affair is by invitation only," he ordered coldly, wanting to get rid of him as quickly as possible.

"I have no intention of staying. I need only to speak with Miss Anderson. I have an important message for her."

"I'm sorry, sir. This is not the time or place. Please leave."

"If you refuse to let me in, could you at least find her and bring her here? I'll wait outside to speak with her," he insisted.

"No, sir. I—"

"Is there a problem, Horace?" Edwin Chase asked as he came to the door.

"No, sir," Horace answered as he shut the door in the rough-looking man's face. He certainly had never seen the man around town, and Mr. Chase's directions at the beginning of the evening had been clear—no one was to be admitted without an invitation. It was a private party with an exclusive guest list.

Dan thought about kicking the door open and walking right on in, but he knew he'd be in for a fight if he did and he didn't want a fight tonight.

He just wanted to find Penny.

Irritated, but not about to give up, Dan went around to the side of the house and saw that there was a balcony off the ballroom. He grasped the rail and quickly swung up and over, grateful for the cover of darkness. Now all he had to do was figure out which woman was Penny.

Chapter Four

The Chase ball was always one of the highlights of the social scene. It was seen as the beginning of the holiday season, and Penny was having a delightful time, visiting with her friends and dancing quite often with several of the young men from town. She was circling the dance floor now in the arms of Jared Montgomery when suddenly Richard appeared and tapped Jared on the shoulder to cut in.

"If I may?" Richard said.

Jared had no choice but to turn her over to the other man.

"Good evening, Penny," Richard said, gazing down at her. He thought Penny was one of the prettiest girls in town, and he definitely liked dancing with her. He was just sorry he'd been late showing up, but he'd had business to attend to and that had to come first.

"Good evening, Richard." She smiled at him, knowing Amanda would be delighted that he was finally there. Her friend had been watching for him ever since they'd arrived and was disappointed when she couldn't find him right away.

"You certainly look lovely this evening," he complimented her.

"Thank you."

They got quiet as they continued to dance and enjoy the moment.

Taking care to stay out of sight by the French doors, Dan kept a vigilant watch over the ballroom. Crowded as it was, it wasn't easy for him to get a good look at everyone. He finally spotted a dark-haired young woman in a turquoise gown. Of all the women there, she bore the closest resemblance to the portrait Jack had given him.

Dan frowned, knowing what he was going to do next wasn't the most pleasant way to make her acquaintance for the first time, but there was nothing else he could do. Without hesitating any longer, Dan stepped forward and opened the French doors to let himself into the ballroom.

"What in the world—" One of the men dancing with his wife near the doors was shocked when a rough-looking stranger wearing work clothes and a cowboy hat walked in unannounced. The man stopped dancing and quickly backed away with his wife, believing the intruder was there to cause trouble.

Dan ignored those who'd turned to look in his direction. He started making his way through the crowd, but he didn't get very far.

A well-dressed man moved directly into his path, blocking his way. "Guests come in through the front door."

Dan knew there was no point in trying to make

any excuses or reason with the man. "I'm not a guest."

"Then I suggest you leave."

A space cleared around them, and the musicians, upon seeing the disruption, stopped playing.

"I'm not here to cause any trouble. I just need to speak with Miss Anderson." Dan glanced in the direction of the woman he thought might be Penny, but she had her back to him. "If you'll excuse me—"

Just as he was turning away to walk over to the young woman, the doorman appeared in the main doorway along with another male servant.

Dan knew he had to reach Jack's daughter before he got tossed out—again. "Miss Anderson?"

Penny hadn't been paying much attention to what was going on, but at the sound of someone calling her name she turned around. She frowned slightly in confusion at the sight of the tall stranger, dressed more for ranch work than a society ball, crossing the ballroom toward her. She had no idea who he was or what he was doing there, but she knew she was going to find out real soon. "Yes, I'm Penny Anderson."

"I need to talk with you for a moment," Dan told her.

Concerned, she started to step forward to speak to him, but Richard caught her by the arm to stop her. "What are you doing? Stay here and let them throw him out. He doesn't belong here. "

"I have to see what he wants," Penny insisted.

Pulling her arm free of Richard's hold, she boldly stepped forward. Tall and broad-shouldered, the cowboy was an impressive figure of a man—and ruggedly handsome. "Who are you? Why are you here?"

From her dark hair and dark eyes that sparkled with intelligence to the elegant blue gown she was wearing, Penny was exactly what Dan thought a fancy eastern lady should look like, and he immediately wondered if he had any chance at all of convincing her to return to the Lazy Ace.

"My name's Dan Roland. I work for your father, and I have news for you from him. Is there some place private where we could talk?" He quickly forced himself to concentrate on his reason for being there.

Penny was about to answer when the doorman grabbed Dan by the shoulder. "You're not going to be doing any talking. You're leaving now, cowboy. Let's go," the servant ordered.

Penny spoke up, not wanting any trouble. "No, wait." Dan Roland wouldn't have gone to so much trouble to speak with her if what he had to say wasn't important. "It's all right. I need to have a few moments with Mr. Roland."

Edwin Chase came up just then to see what was going on. "What's the problem, my dear?"

"There is no problem, Mr. Chase. Mr. Roland traveled all the way from my father's ranch in Texas with some news for me. We need to speak privately, so I was wondering if we could use your parlor?" Penny asked politely.

Edwin looked at the stranger for a moment and was impressed when the intruder met his gaze straight on. He could see no deception or conniving in his regard, and he sensed there was no threat from him. "Come with me."

He had started to lead the way from the ballroom when Matilda demanded, "Penny! What's going on?" She had been sitting with some of her friends at the very back of the ballroom and had missed all of the initial excitement. Only when someone told her of the uninvited cowboy who'd gone after Penny did she get up and rush over to find her niece standing with a tall, impressive man who was no doubt a Texan.

"This is Mr. Roland, Aunt Matilda. He has a message from my father," she quickly explained.

"I'm taking them to the parlor, Matilda. Why don't you come with us?" Edwin suggested.

Matilda went along as their host led them from the ballroom with everyone watching with open interest.

Amanda was standing on the far side of the ballroom when she saw Penny walk out with Mr. Chase, her aunt, and the stranger. She couldn't imagine what was going on. She hurried over to find Richard, who was standing with one of the other men.

"What happened?" Amanda asked as she joined

them. "Who was that man with Penny and her aunt?"

Richard shrugged dismissively. "Something about a message from her father."

"So the man just climbed up on the balcony and came in to find her." The other man added.

Amanda was amazed at the stranger's resourceful determination. "I wonder why he didn't just wait until tomorrow to try to reach her?"

"Who knows?" Richard said. "It doesn't matter. What matters is the musicians are playing again and we're not dancing, Amanda. May I have the honor?" Earlier, he'd been seriously considering courting Penny, but after seeing how she acted with the cowboy, he believed Amanda just might be more to his liking.

"I'd be delighted," Amanda responded. At any other time, being in Richard's arms as he twirled her around the dance floor would have been as close to heaven on earth as she could get. But she was too worried about Penny to fully appreciate the experience. What could have happened?

Edwin Chase took them down the main hall to the front parlor. "I'll leave you to take care of your business. If you need anything—" He looked to Penny, wanting to reassure her.

"Thank you, Mr. Chase." Penny was truly grateful that Dan's unexpected intrusion hadn't caused too much trouble. She didn't want to ruin anyone's good time.

Edwin left the room, but he did not close the hallway door on his way out. He wanted to make sure the ladies were safe, and by leaving it open, his servants would be able to hear if anything went wrong.

Alone at last, Matilda looked up at the stranger, trying to judge his character. "Well, Mr. Roland, what is so important that you had to come barging into the Chases' home this way to see Penny?"

Dan saw the fierce protectiveness she had for her niece. He knew that was a good quality, but it also meant he was going to have to convince not only Penny, but her aunt, too. "I have a letter for Miss Anderson from her father."

He pulled the envelope from his shirt pocket and held it out to her.

Penny hesitated for a moment, looking from the letter to Dan Roland. Their gazes met, and she could see how serious he was. She took the envelope from him, feeling decidedly unsettled by what might be in it. She took a deep breath and pulled out the one-page letter.

Dear Penny,

It is with great sadness that I am sending this letter to you.

I have just learned that I have only a short time left to live and I need to see you again before I pass away. Dan Roland is

my foreman here on the Lazy Ace. He will
accompany you back to the ranch.
With love,
Your father

"What does the letter say?" Matilda asked, noticing how Penny paled as she'd read the missive.
"What does your father want from you?"

Penny lifted her gaze to her aunt, her thoughts
dark and troubled, her heart aching. "I have to
go back to the ranch—"

"No, you don't," her aunt said. "Your life is here
now. Your mother wanted you to stay right here
in the city with me."

"You don't understand, Aunt Matilda—" Her
voice was choked with emotion.

"Understand what?"

"My father needs me," Penny managed. "He's
dying."

"Jack is dying?" Matilda was aghast at the
news. Of all the things she'd suspected Jack was
going to this length to contact Penny about, this
wasn't one of them. The thought that he could
be in such ill health shocked her. She looked to
the man who'd brought the letter to Penny, and
remembering all that Elizabeth had told her about
the harshness of life on the ranch, she demanded,
"What happened to him? Was he shot? Did he
have an accident?"

"No, ma'am," Dan replied. "It was nothing like

that. The doctor told him it was his heart, so I have to get Miss Anderson back to the Lazy Ace as quickly as possible."

Memories overwhelmed Penny as she stood there holding the letter—memories of her father's one short visit to see them there in St. Louis all those years ago and memories of the life she'd led on the Lazy Ace when she'd just been a young girl. Along with those memories came the pain of knowing that he hadn't tried to stay in touch with her very often, even though she'd written to him regularly early on. "Why does he want to see me now after all this time? Why does he suddenly care about me and want me there?"

Dan was gravely serious as he answered her, "He doesn't have long to live, and he wants to see you before—"

"But he never tried to stay in touch with me—"

Dan was caught off guard by her statement. He glanced at her aunt and wasn't surprised to see the older woman quickly avert her eyes and look away from him. He told Penny, "Your father did write to you. He wrote regularly, but he never heard back."

"He didn't write regularly," she denied. "I only got a few letters from him—"

"Maybe you should ask your aunt about that." Dan wondered what had really gone on after seeing Matilda's reaction.

"Aunt Matilda?" Penny turned to look at her, her eyes wide and questioning.

"What, dear?" she responded nervously.

"Is he right? Do you know anything about this?"

"Well—"

"Well, what?" Penny pressed her for the truth.

Matilda met her gaze, feeling decidedly guilty over the deception her mother had started and she had continued. "Your mother always thought it best to keep your contact with your father to a minimum. She wanted you to be happy here, so she made it a point to destroy most of the correspondence he sent you, and, though he wasn't writing as often, I did continue her practice after she passed away."

Chapter Five

Penny was absolutely taken aback by the discovery. She stared at her aunt in shock. "But why? Why would Mother do that? She knew how much I loved my father."

"That's precisely why she did it," Matilda countered a bit harshly. "She didn't want you to go back to the ranch. She wanted to keep you in the city with her, where she knew you would be safe."

Penny couldn't help it. She sank down on the sofa and said nothing for a long moment as she thought about what her mother and her aunt had done. She wanted to cry, but she knew it was pointless. Raw, painful emotions churned within her, and she decided to draw upon those very emotions for the strength she needed to get through this hard time. Finally, she lifted her head to look at her aunt. "I'll be leaving for Texas with Mr. Roland as soon as he can make the arrangements."

"But, Penny—" Matilda wanted to convince her not to go.

The Anderson side of Penny came back to life within her as she stood up to face her aunt. "I'm going, Aunt Matilda. I will need your help to find an appropriate chaperone for the trip," she said, for she knew her aunt would never consider leaving the city to travel with her.

"It'll take us two to three weeks to get back, depending on connections," Dan noted. "I checked the schedule when I arrived in town earlier today, and there is a train leaving late tomorrow afternoon."

"If we can arrange for my chaperone in time, we'll be on that train, Mr. Roland. Where are you staying?" she asked.

"I have a room at the Planter's House Hotel."

"Fine. I'll send word to you in the morning to let you know how arrangements are progressing. I plan to do everything I can to make sure we leave tomorrow."

"I'll wait until I get your message to purchase the tickets." He was relieved she had agreed to come along without a fight, but he also knew she had been hurt by the deception she'd discovered in her life.

"Thank you, Mr. Roland," Penny said.

"I'll be waiting to hear from you in the morning, Miss Anderson." He tipped his hat to them. "Good night, ladies."

Dan left them alone in the parlor to let himself out. He wasn't surprised to find the doorman standing by the front door, but he was surprised when he opened the door for him.

"Good night, sir," the servant said.

"Good night." Dan walked outside to see the driver and carriage still waiting for him.

"Did you get your business all taken care of?" the driver asked.

"Yes. We can go back to the hotel now."

"Yes, sir."

Dan was quiet as they started back to the Planter's House. Things had worked out so far, but they still had a long way to go. He had to get Penny safely back to the ranch to Jack. He couldn't help feeling a little sorry for the girl. With the way her mother and her aunt had deceived her, she'd never had any idea just how much her father loved her and had been missing her. Dan was glad that she would get the chance to be with him again. Not everybody had that opportunity.

Back inside in the parlor, Matilda faced her niece. "Penny, I—"

"No, don't say anything more," Penny said, starting to leave the room, her father's letter still in hand. "I'll be ready to leave as soon as I find Amanda and tell her good-bye."

Matilda was ashamed by all that had transpired, and she relented. "I'll have our carriage brought around."

Penny made her way back to the ballroom and stood in the main doorway looking for her friend. Amanda happened to see her first and came hurrying across the room to find out what was going on.

"You're back!" Amanda said, glad to see her, but worried because her friend looked so serious.

"Not for long," Penny told her. She led them to a quiet corner so they could talk.

"What do you mean?" Amanda asked. "What did that man want with you?"

"His name was Dan Roland and my father sent him here to find me and give me this letter." She looked down at the missive she was still holding. "Amanda—" She lifted her sad gaze to her friend. "My father is very ill. He doesn't have long to live, so I'm going back to Texas. I have to see him again before he dies."

"Oh, Penny—" Amanda hugged her, knowing how the news must have upset her. "Is there anything I can do for you?"

"Just pray, Amanda. Mr. Roland was saying we have to hurry back, so I'll probably be leaving tomorrow if I can arrange for a chaperone to travel with me quickly enough."

"I wish I could be your chaperone," Amanda offered, knowing her friend was going to need all the moral support she could get, to get through the hard times ahead.

"So do I," Penny said.

"Have you told Richard yet?"

"No, I wanted to tell you first."

"Let's go find him."

"All right, but then I'll have to leave. I've got a lot to get done before tomorrow."

Richard was on the dance floor with one of the other young ladies, so they stayed where they were, waiting for the dance to end before approaching him.

Meanwhile, in the corner where the older ladies were sitting, the gossip was quickly spreading. They had seen Penny return, but not Matilda or the cowboy.

"What have you heard?" Louise Gallagher asked as she joined them.

"Nothing yet," Dwylah Carpenter replied. "I wonder where Matilda went with that cowboy. I got a good look at him, and he was real handsome."

"If you like cowboys," one matron said, sneering.

"I do," Dwylah said without hesitation, "and you could probably use one in your life. He'd liven things up for you a bit!"

"Oh!" The other woman was outraged by her remark. "I prefer true gentlemen." She got up to move away.

Dwylah and Louise shared an amused look.

"She doesn't know a good thing when she sees it," Louise told her friend.

"That's fine with me. Then I won't have to fight her for him," she laughed. "I've read some dime novels. I know what heroes those cowboys are—always standing up and doing what's right to save the day—and rescue the heroine. Do you think Matilda might have run off with him?"

"I wouldn't have blamed her."

"Dwylah—here comes Matilda now. She'll tell us what this was all about," Louise said, pointing toward the main door where their friend had just reentered the ballroom.

"It's about time. Our cowboy's not with her, though. I wonder what she did with him?" she chuckled. "She should have brought him back in with her, so I could have claimed him for at least one dance."

They were laughing until Matilda got closer and they saw how dark and serious her expression was. Their mood sobered, for they knew whatever news she had wasn't good.

"I'm afraid Penny and I will have to be leaving soon," Matilda began.

"Why?" Dwylah asked. "The evening's just getting started."

Matilda quickly told her two friends all that had happened. "She desperately wants to leave tomorrow and I can't let her go until I've arranged for a chaperone to make the trip with her."

"Who are you going to get at this late date?" Louise knew it wouldn't be a simple thing to find someone willing and able to leave town on such short notice, especially to travel to some place as uncivilized as Texas.

"I have no idea," Matilda said wearily, sitting down with them to try to collect her thoughts.

Dwylah's eyes lit up. "I know who you can get to be her chaperone."

"Who?"

"I'll go with her."

"You?" Matilda was startled by Dwylah's offer.

"I've always wanted to see the Wild West, and this will be my chance. In fact, it might be my only chance, as old as I'm getting." Dwylah was a widow with ample funds and a very comfortable lifestyle, but she'd always enjoyed a challenge.

Louise was smiling. She knew what an adventurer her friend was. "Dwylah's right, Matilda. She's the perfect one to make the trip with Penny, and who knows, maybe she'll find herself a cowboy while she's out there."

Matilda couldn't believe her friend really wanted to do this, but she knew Dwylah would be fantastic as the chaperone her niece needed. "Are you sure?"

"Yes. I have nothing to keep me here. Penny needs my help, and I'm more than willing to do it."

"And you can be ready tomorrow?"

"It won't be easy to get packed that fast, but I'll do it. When Penny is ready to leave, I'll be with her. I'll make sure she gets to Texas safely."

"I'll pay for your ticket and all your travel expenses and whatever else you need for the trip. And, oh, I almost forgot to tell you, Dan Roland will be traveling with you," Matilda informed her.

"I was hoping you were going to say that." Dwylah smiled in delight. "Now I know I'm going."

Louise couldn't help smiling, too. If nothing else, Dwylah's ability to make people laugh would no doubt help make the long trip seem less arduous for everyone. "I'll miss you."

"Come with us," she challenged.

"No, you're the adventurous one. You go and then come back and tell me all about it."

"I will," she answered, a mischievous twinkle in her eyes.

"Let's go tell Penny," Matilda said. "I'm sure she'll be relieved."

Matilda and Dwylah went to seek Penny out and let her know everything had been arranged.

Richard was a bit startled as he looked down at Penny. "There's no other way for you to handle this?"

"No. It's important that I get to see my father again, and I didn't want to leave without telling you good-bye."

Richard thought about taking her in his arms and kissing her, but this was hardly the place to be so bold, and, besides, Amanda was standing right there with them. "We'll miss you, Penny."

"I'll write Amanda regularly and let her know how things are going."

"Do you think you'll be back by Christmas?" Amanda asked.

She looked uncertain. "There's no way to know what's going to happen once I get there."

Penny didn't get to say any more, for just then

her aunt and her friend Dwylah sought them out.

"Are you ready to leave, Penny?" Aunt Matilda asked, her manner reserved. She knew her niece was very angry and upset with her, and she would have to handle things between them very carefully from now on.

"Yes, Aunt Matilda," she replied. Then looking back at Richard, she said, "Good-bye, Richard."

"Good-bye, Penny."

Penny and Amanda went with the ladies as they made their way from the ballroom. They were all aware that they were being watched quite carefully by the other people in attendance, but they didn't care.

"I'll thank Edwin and Lillian, and then we can go," Matilda said. "Wait for me in the hall."

She saw their host and hostess standing nearby and went to speak with them and to tell them how everything had turned out. A short time later, Matilda came out into the hall where Penny, Amanda, and Dwylah were standing.

"Did you tell her yet, Dwylah?" Matilda asked.

"No," the older woman answered.

"Tell me what?" Penny looked between the two of them in confusion.

"Your aunt and I have everything all figured out, so you'll be able to leave tomorrow," Dwylah explained.

"I will?"

"Yes. I've agreed to be your chaperone on the

trip. I can be ready to leave for Texas as soon as you are."

Penny was stunned and thankful. She had so feared being delayed for days trying to find someone suitable to make the long journey with her.

"Oh, Dwylah, thank you!" Impulsively, she hugged the older woman. "I'll let Mr. Roland know first thing in the morning that we'll be ready to travel whenever he is."

"We'd better go, dear. You have a lot of packing to do," Matilda said. "Dwylah, we'll send word to you as soon as we hear back from Mr. Roland, but plan on departing on an afternoon train."

"I will."

Matilda and Penny left the Chase mansion to head home.

Penny knew she wouldn't get much rest that night.

Chapter Six

As exhausted as he was, Dan had thought he would fall asleep right away. It had been weeks since he'd had a clean bed to sleep in, but he had too much on his mind to be able to completely relax and enjoy the comfort of the room. His thoughts were racing as he tried to imagine how long it would take Penny and her aunt to hire a chaperone to accompany her on the trip. He hoped not long, but he'd never had to deal with this kind of situation before.

Dan stared up at the ceiling, wondering again how Penny and her mother could ever have left Jack and the Lazy Ace the way they had. After what he'd experienced in life, he knew how important it was to have a real home and a family.

Dan wondered, too, how Penny would fare on the long trip to the ranch. The train travel wouldn't be bad, but that was a very small part of the overall journey. Covering the long miles across Texas in the cramped stagecoaches in cold weather was going to be a rough time for her and her chaperone—there was no doubt about that.

He tried to imagine Penny living on the ranch again after all these years of being in the city, and he knew it wasn't going to be easy for her.

Even so, he didn't care. His job was to make sure she got there safely, and he would do it . . . for Jack's sake.

Dan finally managed to fall asleep, but it wasn't a deep sleep. He came awake again just as the eastern sky started to lighten and decided he might as well get up. He'd just finished getting dressed when a knock came at his door.

"Who is it?"

"Charley, the desk clerk."

Dan opened the door to see what he wanted at such an early hour.

"I have a message for you here from a Miss Anderson," the clerk said as he handed him a small envelope.

Dan gave him a tip for his trouble and shut the door to quickly read the message.

Dear Mr. Roland,

All the arrangements have been made. My chaperone and I will be ready to depart whenever you are. Please let me know as soon as possible when you need us to be ready.

Sincerely,

Penny Anderson

With great relief at the good news, he grabbed up his coat and left the hotel to get the tickets for the afternoon train and to send a wire to Jack letting him know they were on their way.

The days ahead would be challenging, but he believed the hardest part of his trip was over.

Jack's daughter had agreed to return home.

Penny finished packing the last of the clothes she was going to take with her in her two suitcases. This had been her home for a long time now, and she found herself wondering if she would ever be back here again. Tears threatened, but she refused to cry. She was doing what she had to do. Right then, seeing her father again was the most important thing.

She could only imagine how long and rough the trip was going to be, but with Dwylah along, she knew their time together wouldn't be dull. Drawing a deep breath to fortify herself, Penny got up and left the room. Mr. Roland had sent a note to meet him at the train station at one o'clock. And there was still one more thing she had to do before then. She found her aunt in the parlor, waiting for her.

"I'm ready to go to the cemetery now," Penny said.

"Let me get Andrew. I told him earlier that we were going there some time this morning."

A few minutes later, Andrew, the cook's husband, drove their small carriage around front to pick them up. The drive to the cemetery didn't take long.

Matilda waited back in the carriage as Penny

descended and headed toward her mother's grave. She knew her niece needed some time alone there.

Penny stared down at the marker as if it would give her the answers she sought. "Why did you keep Papa's letters from me?" she whispered.

A chilling wind picked up, and Penny clutched her coat more tightly around her.

"Good-bye, Mama," she said softly.

She took one last look around and then returned to the carriage. The driver helped her back in, and she sat down beside her aunt again.

"Are you ready?" Matilda asked.

Penny nodded. "We need to get back before Dwylah and Mr. Roland show up."

"We can go now, Andrew," she ordered.

They started the trip back to the house.

In her heart as the cemetery disappeared from view, Penny wondered how long it would be before she came back to visit her mother's grave again.

They'd been riding in silence for a while when Matilda finally spoke up.

"I can't believe you're leaving."

"Neither can I. Everything happened so fast."

"I'm going to miss you, and with Christmas coming . . ." It saddened her to know Penny wouldn't be there for the holidays.

"I'll be with Papa this Christmas." The thought warmed her heart. She was so glad that she was being given the opportunity to set things right between them. She knew she had a lot to make up for, and she was going to get the chance.

"Yes, you will."

They fell silent again.

Dwylah had made it a point to arrive at Matilda's house early, and she'd been keeping a sharp eye out the front parlor window ever since, watching for Dan Roland to arrive. The minute she saw his carriage pull up, she headed for the front door to let him in. There was no need to bother Matilda and Penny as they made their final preparations. She was about to travel across the country with this handsome young cowboy, and she was eager to see him again and to get to know him.

Deep in her heart, Dwylah realized this was a sad time for Penny, but she was determined to try to keep the young woman's spirits up as best she could during the trip. She had even spoken to Matilda about the possibility that she would stay on with her for a while once they'd reached the ranch, just to make sure Penny didn't feel alone and lost.

"It's about time you got here!" Dwylah threw open the front door just as he reached the top step.

"Am I late?" Dan was surprised by the older woman's welcome. He had no idea who the short, silver-haired woman was, and he immediately worried that something had gone wrong.

"Heavens, no," Dwylah said. "I've just been waiting to get to meet you, that's all. Come on in."

She stepped back as Dan took off his hat and came into the front hall.

"I saw you last night, but didn't get the chance to talk to you," she went on, giving him a big smile. "I'm Dwylah—the chaperone."

"It's nice to meet you, Miss Dwylah. I'm Dan Roland."

"I know who you are, young man," she laughed. "Don't just stand there. Come on in where it's warm." She grabbed him by the arm and drew him farther into the house before shutting the door behind him. She gazed up at him, happy to be getting her first real good, up-close look at him. She was pleased to find that her first impression had proven true. He was one handsome man with his dark hair and eyes and lean, hard jawline. She had no doubt he was a force to be reckoned with.

"I want to hear all about you on this trip. You must have some great stories to tell us about living out West."

"There might be a few," he answered good-naturedly.

"Only a few?" There was a twinkle of mischief in her eyes.

"Only a few that are suitable for ladies such as yourself," he answered.

"I'll be looking forward to hearing them." She was hoping she could get some of the wilder tales out of him, too, before their long trip was over. She always did like finding out the real truth about things.

"Is Miss Anderson ready to go?"

"Yes, she is. We're all packed up." She gestured toward their bags there in the hall near the bottom of the staircase. "Let me go see if I can find her, and I'll let her know you're here."

Dwylah had just started off down the hall when Penny and her aunt came out from the back of the house.

"I'm here, Dwylah," Penny told her.

"Miss Anderson," Dan greeted her, and nodded to her aunt. "Ma'am."

Matilda, taking charge of the moment. "Hello, Mr. Roland. I see you've met Dwylah already. Has she told you that she'll be traveling with you as Penny's chaperone?"

"Yes, ma'am."

"She'll also be staying on with Penny for as long as necessary once you get to the ranch."

"That'll be fine," he said. "I'd better get these bags loaded up so we can get over to the station."

"I can get Andrew to do that—" Matilda began.

"No need." Dan put his hat back on and quickly picked up several of the bags to carry out to the waiting carriage and driver.

Dwylah knew the moment of their departure had come, and she followed her cowboy outside to give Penny and Matilda time to say their good-byes in private. With all the tears that were about to be shed, she understood why Matilda didn't want to go to the station with them to see them off.

"Penny, darling, please be careful," Matilda bid her when they were alone.

"I will."

She embraced her niece warmly. She loved her and everything she'd ever done had been because she'd wanted her safe and happy. "I'm going to miss you."

"I'll miss you, too."

"Tell your father . . ." She paused, not sure what would be appropriate after all this time. "Tell him I'll be praying for you both."

"Thank you." Penny didn't say anything more as Dan came back in the house just then to get the last of their luggage.

Matilda was openly weeping now, and Dwylah was definitely teary-eyed.

"Good-bye, Penny." She kissed her one last time on the cheek and walked with her out to the carriage. When Dan finished loading the last of the luggage, she said to him, "You make sure she's safe."

"I will," Dan promised, his expression serious.

He helped Penny up into the carriage with the chaperone and then climbed up to sit beside the driver on the driver's bench.

"We'll wire you as soon as we get there," Dwylah told Matilda.

"I'll be waiting to hear from you."

"Good-bye, Aunt Matilda," Penny called to her as the carriage started to move away.

Penny was as prepared as she would ever be for the long journey to come. "It's going to be a long trip."

"Yes, it is," Dwylah agreed, "but as long as the weather stays clear, we should be able to make it without too much trouble."

A flash of pain was mirrored in Penny's eyes for a moment as she looked at her friend. "I hope so. I really need to see my father again."

"You will, dear," she reassured her. "You'll be with him for Christmas. I can't imagine that he'd like any present better than having you with him."

"Being with Papa is going to be my best present, too."

They sat back, and Penny realized how thankful she was that her father hadn't given up and had sent Dan Roland to find her.

Chapter Seven

Dan was glad to be leaving St. Louis. Things had worked out just as he'd hoped and now it was just a matter of keeping Penny and Miss Dwylah safe and out of trouble on their cross-country trek. Safe, he hoped wouldn't be a problem. But he had a feeling it would be a challenge to keep Dwylah out of trouble. The train depot was crowded, and he kept the ladies with him as he went to check in with the clerk.

"Is the train on time?" Dan asked.

"It should be pulling out real soon. Once everything is loaded up, you'll be on your way."

"Thanks." Dan was looking forward to the day when the railroad made it all the way to Sagebrush, but it wasn't going to happen any time soon.

"So it's really going to take more than two weeks?" Dwylah asked.

"If we don't have any trouble," Dan assured her.

"This is my first trip to Texas," she said. "How far do we go on the train?"

"Just to Tipton. From there on, we'll be on a stagecoach the rest of the way," Dan told her.

"It *is* going to be a long trip," Dwylah remarked.

She'd heard stories of how harsh the conditions on stages could be.

"Are you sure you want to do this?" Penny asked, knowing this was Dwylah's last chance to back out.

"Of course," the chaperone said with a smile to reassure her. "I'm going with you, no matter what. You know I always like a challenge."

When the call came that it was time to board, they got ready to get on the train.

Dan was the last one to board. He had started to get on when he saw a young boy dash across the street about half a block away. There looked to be a man and several other boys chasing him, so he figured the boy had gotten into some kind of trouble. He knew all about that from his own days of living on the streets after he'd run away from the orphanage. He thought about going after the boy to try to help, but there was no time. The train was about to pull out. Dan got onboard and went to sit on the seat facing the one where the women were sitting.

Dwylah was quite delighted when their handsome escort sat down right across from her. She smiled to herself thinking she wouldn't get bored being forced to watch him the whole way. She had noticed earlier when he'd come to the house to pick them up that he'd been wearing his gun belt, so she asked, "Since you're wearing your gun today, are you expecting trouble?"

"You never know when you're traveling. It never hurts to be ready, just in case," he told her.

"Should Penny and I be carrying guns, too? I mean, we are heading into the Wild West."

"No, ma'am," he said. Knowing she was teasing, he smiled at her. "That's why I'm here. I'll keep you safe."

"I believe you will," she agreed. "But if you ever need any help, I do have my knitting needles with me." She laughed. "You never know when they might just come in handy."

"I'll remember that, Miss Dwylah," Dan promised, knowing she would be dangerous with her needles.

"I know you're being respectful, but just call me Dwylah, because from now on I'm going to start calling you Dan. We're going to be spending a lot of time together, and we might as well get used to each other. Right, Penny?"

"You're right, Dwylah," she answered, looking to Dan. "And you can just call me Penny."

"All right, Penny—Dwylah, it looks like we're on our way," he said as the train jerked into motion and started to move out.

They sat back, seeking what little comfort they could find on the hard seats.

"So, we've only got about two weeks to go until you're home," Dwylah said to Penny.

"Two weeks . . ." Penny repeated softly, and she turned to gaze out the train window for a last look at the city that had been her home for quite a while now.

The Reverend Nick Miller was frowning as he stood on the corner of the street staring after the train as it pulled out of the station.

"Reverend Miller!"

Nick gave a shake of his head and returned his focus to the two boys who'd accompanied him.

"What is it, Joey?" he asked.

"We found Steve," the boy said, pointing down the filthy dead-end alley.

"You two wait here for me."

Nick strode through the alley to where Steve was trying to hide and knelt beside the frightened six-year-old. "There's no need to be afraid."

He put a comforting hand on the boy's shoulder and could feel him shaking and weeping in silence.

"Joey and Marty are here with me," he tried again. "We were worried about you when we couldn't find you this morning."

Nick felt the tension and the fight drain out of the boy. With one last sob, Steve threw himself into Nick's arms. Nick scooped him up and carried him out of the alley back to where the other boys were waiting.

"Is he all right?" Marty and Joey asked.

"He's tired, but he'll be fine," Nick told them. "Let's get him on back home."

"The orphanage isn't my home!" Steve lifted his head defiantly, the look in his eyes tortured.

"I know how you feel, Steve. Believe me, I know," Nick said.

Steve had been at the orphanage since the death of his parents several months before. Nick knew he was alone in the world now, and afraid—so very afraid. The coming holiday season would be his first without his family, and Nick understood how being at the home only magnified the pain and loneliness the orphaned boys experienced.

As they started back to the orphanage, Nick glanced one last time in the direction of the train station and then shook his head. That couldn't have been Danny getting on that train. It still pained Nick to think of his lost brother. He hadn't seen or heard from Danny in all these years. He'd never known what had happened to him, and that was why he had followed his calling to become a pastor and to work at an orphanage. He cared deeply for the boys. He wanted to give them a place where they would know they were loved.

Nick looked down at little Steve and offered up a silent prayer that he could find some way to win the boy's trust and help heal his pain. His own adoptive parents had helped him through the hard times, and he wanted to be there for these boys to give them whatever support they needed to grow up to be good, upstanding, honorable young men.

It was a long walk back to the orphanage, but they made it. Miss Lawson, one of the teachers, saw them coming and hurried to open the door and let them in.

"You found him!" she exclaimed in delight.

"Thanks to Marty and Joey," Nick told her as he set Steve on his feet before her.

Miss Lawson hugged both Marty and Joey. "Good job." Then she turned to speak with Steve. "Thank heaven you're back. I was so worried about you."

Steve lifted his head to look at the tall, thin, gray-haired teacher. She was one of the strictest teachers there at the home, and to find out she'd been worried about him, surprised him. "You were?"

"Why, yes. You're my best speller. What would I do without you in class, young man? You set the example for all the other younger boys."

Steve had never had any open praise in his life for his studies. He was taken aback by her words. "I do?"

"Yes, you do, and don't forget it. Come see me when you've finished talking with Reverend Miller and I'll go over the assignments you missed today so you won't fall behind in your studies. All right?"

Steve nodded. "Yes, ma'am."

Nick was impressed with her handling of the situation. "Joey, Marty, I'll see you two at dinner. Steve, come with me."

Steve followed the reverend into his small office off the main hall. He stood before Reverend Miller's desk, his head hanging in shame, his shoulders stooped with weariness.

Nick sat down at his desk and looked at the boy. "You can sit down, Steve."

Steve looked up, shocked. Usually when anyone got in trouble at the home, their punishment was strict. He'd been expecting to be spanked. "I can?"

"Yes."

He quickly sat in one of the two chairs positioned in front of the reverend's desk and waited to see what Reverend Miller was going to say.

Nick saw the puzzlement in his expression. "I know you're going through a hard time right now, Steve. This time of year with the holidays coming . . . Well, it's hard to be without your family. I know, because I've been there myself."

"You have?"

"I was orphaned at a young age, just like you," Nick explained, and he went on to tell him of his time at the orphanage. "It was traumatic for me to be taken from my older brother, Danny, and I ran away from my adopted home to go back to find my brother. When I got there, though, Danny was gone. It turned out my brother had run off to try to find me, and I was returned to my adopted family. I stayed with them after that."

"You're lucky to have a brother," Steve said.

"I know, but I haven't seen him since then."

"He never came back? He never found you?"

"No."

"What do you think happened to him?"

"I don't know, and that's why I was so worried about you. It's dangerous being on the streets alone." Nick met his gaze. "Where did you think you were going?"

The boy looked shamed. "I don't know. I just didn't want to be here. I wanted to go home." His eyes widened as if the truth just came to him. "But I don't have a home anymore."

Nick saw the change in him and knew the boy had taken a big and painful step toward manhood right then. "Yes, you do, Steve. Your home is right here with us now."

"Yes, sir."

"If you need help with anything, you come find me."

Steve didn't say anything for a moment. Then he asked, "Do you think you'll ever find your brother?"

"It's interesting you should ask that."

"Why?"

"When I was following you, I saw a man who looked a little like what Danny probably would have looked like as a grown-up, getting on the train down at the train station."

"You did?" The boy's eyes widened in amazement at his words. "What did you do? Did you go talk to him?"

"No, no. There was no time. I had to find you, and, besides, he was about a block away from me and the train was getting ready to pull out. I was probably just thinking about Danny because I was worrying about finding you."

"Reverend Miller—"

Nick looked at him questioningly.

"I'm sorry I ran off today. It won't happen again—I promise."

"Good, and thank you, Steve. You can go on and get ready for dinner."

Steve got up and started to leave the office, but he paused at the door to look back at him. "Reverend Miller?"

"Yes, Steve?"

"You ought to go see if you can find out who was riding on that train today. What if it really was your brother? What if he was there and you didn't try to find him again? It's not too late. You could go bring him back. He's probably still worrying about you, too."

Nick didn't want to even think about the possibility. It had been so long, and there had been so much pain involved in losing Danny the way he had. He'd always feared that something terrible had happened to him, and that was why he'd become so serious about helping the homeless, abandoned children he found on the city streets. "I'll have to see."

"Yes, sir."

With that, Steve left the office and closed the door behind him.

Alone, Nick turned to stare out the window, wondering if there was any hope at all that the cowboy could have been his brother.

Chapter Eight

Nick finished the work in his office for the evening and decided to stop by the small chapel to pray for a while before retiring for the night. He was lost in deep meditation when he heard the chapel door open and someone else come into the room. He didn't look up, but continued to offer up his prayers until the person slipped into the pew right beside him. Only then did he glance over, and he was surprised to see that it was Miss Lawson.

"Is something wrong?" he asked, knowing it was unusual for her to come to the chapel at this time of night.

"That's why I'm here," she replied. "You tell me."

He frowned as he faced her. "What do you mean?"

"I mean, Steve just came to find me. He wanted to talk to me about what happened today."

"He did?" Nick was surprised that the youth had managed to sneak out of the sleeping room without being caught. He was one resourceful young man. "What did he say?"

"It was quite interesting, actually," she began, and then hesitated. "Do you want to talk in here or go out in the hall?"

"This is fine," he told her. Since there was no one else in the chapel with them, they wouldn't be disturbing anyone.

"Well, Steve told me about the conversation the two of you had in your office, and he's worried."

"What's he worried about?" Nick was truly concerned. He hadn't thought the boy felt threatened in any way.

"He's worried about you," the prim teacher explained.

"Me?" He was completely caught off guard by her answer.

She nodded. "Evidently you told him a little about your own childhood, and then he said you saw someone who resembled your brother today." She saw the sudden change in his expression.

"Why would that bother him?"

"Steve is a good, sensitive child at heart. Being alone in the world, he understands how wonderful it would be to discover you still had some family." Miss Lawson met Nick's gaze straight on. "Steve wants you to go check with the people at the train station and find out if that man was your brother."

Nick gave a slow shake of his head and managed a wry half smile. "I was just praying about that and wondering what to do."

"It looks like your prayer was answered. Go to the station and check. See if they'll tell you who was on the train. If it wasn't your brother, there's nothing lost. But if it was your brother . . . " "

"I can't even let myself hope that it really could have been Danny," he said quickly. "Not after all this time."

"Oh, ye of little faith," she countered. "Don't ever give up hope. Do it. I'll be glad to go with you, if you'd like, and I'm sure Steve would like to go along, too."

Nick was trying hard to control the glimmer of hope that was burning within him. "It's just after looking for him all those years ago, I was afraid something terrible had happened to him, that he was dead. I never found a trace of him anywhere in the city after he disappeared from the orphanage."

"You can't pass up this chance. It may turn out to be nothing, but what if it really was your brother?" She looked up at him again, her gaze challenging as it met his.

"All right." Nick gave in to her urging. "I'll go."

"Good. What time will we be leaving?"

He was surprised that she really wanted to accompany him. "After the morning prayer service."

"Fine. I'll let Steve know first thing. He'll be excited for you."

"Bring him along," Nick said, knowing without the boy's concern he wouldn't be going to check.

"I will."

Nick stayed on in the chapel for a little while longer. Offering a prayer of thanksgiving for all the blessings in his life and a prayer asking for the fortitude he would need to deal with whatever he found out about the stranger the following day.

It was late, well after midnight, when the train reached Tipton. Dan gathered their bags and hired a carriage to take them to a hotel in town. The hotel wasn't fancy, but it was far cleaner than the way stations they would be sleeping at for the rest of the trip. He saw Penny and Dwylah safely to their rooms and then bedded down himself. He'd considered going to one of the saloons a few streets over for a drink, but he decided against it. He wanted to stay close to the women, just in case they needed him.

Dan got up early so he could check at the stage office to find out how soon they could leave for Sagebrush. The news was good. There was a stage heading out before noon. He booked their passage and returned to the hotel to let the women know when they would be leaving.

Penny was wearing a fashionable traveling gown, looking quite the lady, and he couldn't help wondering how she was going to fare on the rough stagecoach ride. "I was just down at the stage office and found out our stage will be leaving later this morning. We've got time for breakfast and then we'll have to get on down there."

Dwylah spoke up. "A good breakfast sounds wonderful."

"Yes, it does," Penny agreed.

Dan escorted them to the small dining room in the hotel. The food was delicious eggs and hotcakes, bacon and biscuits. They ate hungrily, especially after Dan warned them about the quality of food they would be served at the way stations. They wanted to enjoy a good meal while they could. After packing up their suitcases again, they checked out of the hotel and made their way to the stage office, ready to continue their journey.

Dwylah was delighted when she discovered they were the only passengers on the stage. She sat beside Penny and kept a close eye on Dan as they got as comfortable as they could. The driver checked on them one last time before climbing up to his bench with the man who was riding shotgun with him. The stagecoach jerked into motion, and they were on their way to Texas. They had blankets to use in case they needed them, and they put the leather window coverings down to keep the cold air out.

"It's so nice that we're all by ourselves today," Dwylah remarked. They had had no real time alone with Dan yet, and she was interested in learning more about him.

"Enjoy it while you can, because it won't last," Dan told them. "Usually there are seven or eight people crammed in the stage."

"That would be awkward," Penny agreed, trying to imagine sitting so close to strangers.

"Well, I wouldn't mind sitting close to you or Dan. We'll just have to make sure we do that if anyone else gets on," Dwylah added. Then she looked at Dan and came right out to ask, "All right, Dan Roland. Here I am running off to Texas with you and I don't know a thing about you. Tell me all about yourself. We've got a lot of time to talk now."

"There's not a lot to tell."

"Of course there is. Where are you from originally? Did you grow up in Texas?"

"No. My parents were from Tennessee. My father wanted to go west."

"Where did they end up settling down?" Penny asked.

"We didn't." Dan kept his expression guarded. "My mother died on the way, leaving my dad with me and my younger brother to take care of."

"Oh, how tragic!" Dwylah exclaimed. "How old were you when it happened?"

"I was just twelve and my brother, Nick, was nine."

"That must have been so hard for the two of you," Penny sympathized. "I know what it feels like to lose your mother, and you and your brother were so young."

"It was hard," he agreed.

"So where did your father take you?" Dwylah wondered, and she was surprised by his answer.

"He took us to an orphanage and left us there."

"He did what?" Dwylah's outrage rang through her voice. "But you were only babies!"

Dan met her gaze. "Not for long."

"Did he come back for you?" Penny asked hopefully.

"No. We never heard from him again."

"I'm sorry," Dwylah said. "But despite all your hardship, you've grown into a fine young man, Dan."

"Why, thank you," he said, giving her a warm smile. "Not everything has been hardship. I've got a good job on the Lazy Ace."

"Where's your brother?" Penny asked.

"I don't know," Dan answered. With his having just visited the site of the orphanage, the pain of missing Nick was real within him again.

"You don't know? What happened to separate you?" Dwylah asked.

"Nick was adopted from the orphanage—"

"And you weren't?" Dwylah sounded as though she wanted to take on the adoptive parents herself. Dan had no doubt she'd give them quite the earful if she could.

"No."

"That's terrible!" Penny cried.

"I didn't find out until Nick was already gone. We hadn't been at the orphanage very long when it happened. I'd been doing fieldwork and when I got back from working, the headmistress gave me the news that Nick had been adopted by a family who only wanted one boy."

"You didn't even get the chance to say good-bye?"

"No. They probably figured we'd give them trouble if they did let us see each other again."

"Did you ever try to find him?"

"Oh yeah. I ran away that very night to look for him, but I couldn't find any trace of him or the Miller family who'd adopted him."

"What did you do?" Penny questioned.

"Once I realized I wasn't going to find Nick, I knew there was no going back. I've been on my own ever since."

"You should be very proud of yourself," Dwylah said.

He shrugged slightly. "I did what I had to do."

He still remembered the hard times he had finding a way to survive all those years ago. It hadn't been easy, but he'd done it.

"It's a shame you lost each other that way," Dwylah said. "Maybe one of these days you'll find each other again."

"After all these years, I doubt it. What about you? How did you end up being our chaperone?"

"I'm a widow. My husband died when we were still young, and I've never found another man to take his place."

"You don't have any children?"

"No, and I regret that a lot these days, but I can't change it. As for how I came to be your chaperone—well, I'll tell you," she began, her expression turning mischievous, "when I heard you were the one taking Penny back to her father, I knew I had to make the trip."

"You did?" Dan was surprised.

"The night of the ball when you walked in there, unannounced, determined to find Penny and give her Jack's message—well, I knew right then and there that you were a very special young man. There aren't many men out there who take the risk that you did to find her."

"I had to do it for Jack." He was a little embarrassed by her praise. No one had ever complimented him this way before.

"And you did," she continued. "I'd say, you're not only Jack's foreman, you're his friend."

"That's true enough," Dan remarked; then he looked at Penny. "Your father is a hardworking, honorable man."

"And we're going to get to see him real soon," Dwylah told Penny cheerfully. "Well, almost real soon. How many more days do we have to go, Dan?"

"At least twelve more," he answered. He found himself growing fonder of their chaperone with every passing mile. He couldn't believe Dwylah hadn't remarried. She was certainly a delight now, and he could only imagine what she'd been like thirty years before. "I'll have you and Penny safely back to the Lazy Ace just as soon as possible."

Chapter Nine

Nick concluded the morning prayer service and said a blessing over the children as they got ready to file from the chapel. His heart was filled with love for them as he watched them leave. He followed the children out into the hall to find Miss Lawson and Steve waiting for him.

"Are you ready to go?" Steve asked eagerly.

"Yes. I'm ready."

"This is so exciting!" Steve smiled widely as he looked up at him. "Aren't you excited?"

Nick was so used to being disappointed at moments like these that he'd learned to control his eagerness. Steve's enthusiasm, though, touched him, and he smiled down at the boy. "Yes, Steve. I am."

"Then let's go!" Miss Lawson encouraged.

The trip to the train station didn't take too long, and Nick was glad to find there was a clerk on duty.

"Where you heading?" the clerk asked.

Nick stepped forward to talk to him. "We don't need tickets, I just wanted to ask about a passenger who left town yesterday on the afternoon train."

"What about?" he hedged, leery about giving out private information on his customers.

Nick knew what he was thinking and offered, "I'm Reverend Miller from the Children's Home. I saw a man boarding the train who might have been my brother—"

"Your brother?"

"That's right. I was wondering if you could check and see if Danny Roland was one of the passengers."

"If your name's Miller and his name's Roland, how could he be your brother?" the clerk questioned.

Nick told him the truth. "My real name is Roland, but I was adopted. Danny wasn't."

"Oh." The clerk pulled out the ledger. "You say it was the afternoon departure?"

"Yes."

The clerk paged through until he got to the passenger list for the afternoon train.

"Let's see here . . ." He quickly read through the list of those who'd booked passage that day. "There were two ladies, several married couples, and—" The clerk looked up at him. "Why, yes—here it is. There was a Dan Roland on the train."

Nick was shocked. "It really was Danny!"

Steve let out a yell and all but jumped up and down beside him in his excitement. "I told you to ask! I told you to!"

Nick couldn't help himself. He grabbed up the boy and gave him a quick hug. "Yes, you did, Steve! Yes, you did!"

Miss Lawson was equally excited for Nick, but she managed not to jump around like Steve had done. "This is wonderful news!"

Nick looked at her, all the wild, tumultuous emotions he was feeling showing in his expression. "Yes, it is." He turned back to the clerk. "Thank you. Could you tell me where he was headed?"

"He was booked to Tipton."

"Is there any way of knowing if that was his final destination?"

"As a matter of fact, he was asking me about the fastest way to get to Texas. He was heading to some place called Sagebrush, but there ain't no trains heading anywhere near Sagebrush."

"Sagebrush?" Nick repeated, having never heard of the town before. "How far is it?"

"As I recall, from what he said, he'll be lucky if he makes it there in two weeks."

Steve stepped up and asked, "When's the next train leaving so he can get to Sagebrush, too?"

"You think he's eager to get there, sonny?"

"Yes, sir," Steve answered respectfully.

The clerk quickly checked. "The next train will be late tomorrow afternoon." He glanced at the man standing before him. "You want to book a seat, Reverend?"

"Yes, I do." Nick's determination was real, but he wasn't sure how he would handle things at the Children's Home. He glanced at Miss Lawson. "Do you think we can get things organized at the home that fast?"

Miss Lawson didn't hesitate. "Of course we can. We'll find a way to take care of things while you're gone. You can't miss this chance to find your brother after all these years."

"You're right." Nick smiled at her and looked to the clerk. "Yes, I'll take a ticket for tomorrow. How much will it be?"

The clerk told him the price, and he promised to bring the payment back later that day.

As they left the depot, Nick noticed young Steve had become unusually quiet, scuffing along in the road beside them. Nick stopped walking.

"What is it?" Miss Lawson asked.

"There's one other thing I should have done."

"What?"

"I'll be right back. Wait here for me," Nick directed.

He left them standing there as he went back up the street to the stage office and then came back a few moments later.

"There. Everything's taken care of."

"What did you forget?" Miss Lawson asked.

"I forgot to tell the clerk that I needed a second ticket."

"A second ticket? What for?"

"Because Steve is going with me on this trip,"

he announced, looking down at the boy affectionately. "If he hadn't run off yesterday, I wouldn't
have been at the depot when Danny was boarding
the stage, and then later, Steve was the one who
convinced me to check and see if the man really
had been Danny."

Steve's eyes had widened in disbelief at his
words. "You're gonna take me with you? Really?"

"Yes, son. I'm going to take you with me, if you
want to go. I owe this all to you, and I want you to
come along and help me find my brother in Sagebrush. Are you willing?"

"Yes, sir!"

"I guess we'd better get back to the home and
get everything organized so we can be away this
long—especially with Christmas coming." Nick
was concerned about the other children, but he
knew taking Steve with him would help ease the
pain of the boy's first Christmas without his family.

"I'm sure everything will work out just fine,"
Miss Lawson assured him.

"I hope you're right," Nick said.

"She is! We're going to Texas," Steve said, eager for their adventure to begin.

"Yes, we are." Nick just hoped he'd be able to
track Danny down once they reached the town
of Sagebrush.

It was midafternoon, and the stagecoach had only
been on the road for a few hours when it stopped
in a small town to pick up more passengers. The

time of privacy Penny, Dan, and Dwylah had enjoyed was over.

"Come on, Dan. Get over here with us. There's room for you," Dwylah said.

She scooted over so Dan could sit between them, and he quickly switched sides. Dwylah had liked looking at him, but she enjoyed sitting by him even more. She certainly appreciated his warmth beside her.

Penny was not immune to Dan's nearness, either. A shiver went through her that had nothing to do with the cold as Dan settled in next to her. Their shoulders were touching and the long, lean, powerful length of his leg was pressed against hers. She glanced up at him, to find him looking down at her, and for a moment, their gazes met.

"Am I crowding you? Do you have enough room?" Dan asked, very much aware of her soft, feminine presence beside him. A part of him wanted to slip an arm around her and draw her even closer. She was one pretty woman, but his job was to keep her safe.

"I'm fine," Penny managed.

"I'm fine, too," Dwylah put in.

The new passengers, a married couple, got on and sat down. After exchanging greetings, everyone fell silent as the stage pulled out of town. They all knew they had a long, hard ride ahead of them.

And a hard ride it was.

Dan was finding it difficult to ignore Penny, and it only got worse when the stage took a hard turn and hit a deep rut. The sudden violent lurch of the stagecoach caught Penny unaware and she was thrown forward. Only Dan's quick action in snaring her around the waist and hauling her back against him kept her from falling to the floor.

"Penny! Are you all right?" Dwylah had been shaken by what had happened, but had managed to keep her own seat. She looked over to where Dan was still holding Penny on his lap.

Penny found herself clinging to Dan and trembling from the shock of her unexpected fall. "I think so. Thanks to Dan." She was very aware of his powerful arms around her and she wanted nothing more than to stay right there. She was perfectly safe as long as he was holding her.

Dan's eyes were dark as he looked down at her. "Are you sure?" The last thing he wanted to do was loosen his hold, but for propriety's sake he needed to let her go.

"Yes," she said a little nervously, slipping off his lap and moving to sit beside him again.

"You weren't fooling when you told us riding in the stage was going to be a lot rougher than riding on the train," Dwylah declared.

"It's not easy," he said, giving her a half smile. He was again glad that Dwylah's presence distracted him from the feel of having Penny in his arms. The memory of her soft curves crushed against him was going to be hard to put from his mind.

"You're right about that," Penny agreed. Now she was even more aware of him as a man, of the protective strength of his arms around her and being held against his hard-muscled chest. "I guess I'd better hold on to something from now on."

"Grab Dan," Dwylah said, smiling at her. "We know he's not going to let you fall."

With her chaperone's approval, Penny did just that, holding on to Dan's arm for the next few miles until the road finally evened out.

Dan had been all too aware of Penny's touch, but he'd forced himself to concentrate on the real reason he was there with her. He had to get her back to the ranch, to Jack. At the thought of his friend, his mood grew more serious. Getting her home was all that mattered. He just wished the stage could move faster.

It was almost dark when they finally pulled up at the way station.

"We're here!" the driver shouted as he brought the team to a stop. He jumped down to open the door for the passengers while the man riding shotgun went to see about unloading their bags.

The married couple got out first. Dan climbed down and turned to help Penny and Dwylah descend, while the driver went to take care of the horses. Dan could tell the women were tired already, and he could just imagine how they would be feeling the following night after spending close to twelve hours of travel crammed in the crowded stagecoach.

"Everybody, go on inside," the driver directed. "Vic, the station manager, will have a meal ready for you real soon."

And Vic did.

The dinner wasn't fancy. The food was served on tin plates, but the biscuits were good and the stew was filling. When everyone had finished eating, the women went into the back bedroom to bed down while the men slept in the main room.

"This is certainly not the most luxurious of accommodations," Dwylah said wryly, eyeing the rope cots, pillows, and worn blankets that had been provided and wondering how she would ever manage to fall asleep.

Margaret, the married woman who was traveling with them, laughed. "Compared to some of the way stations I've slept at over the years, this one isn't too bad."

Penny agreed, "I know. I still remember some of the places we stayed at when my mother took me to St. Louis six years ago."

"This is an adventure," Dwylah declared, picking one of the cots for her own and sitting down to test its comfort. When she found there was no comfort, she wasn't surprised. "The important thing is that we get there all safe and sound, and I'm sure we will with Dan taking care of us."

"Is Dan your son?" Margaret asked, for she hadn't seen a wedding ring on the younger woman's hand.

"Oh no, but I would be proud to claim him as my own. I'm Penny's chaperone, and Dan works for her father. We're on our way back to their ranch in Texas," she replied.

"You have a long trip ahead of you."

"Yes, we do. How far are you traveling?" Penny asked.

"Just two more days and we'll be home. I hope you make good time and get there before the weather turns."

"So do we," Penny agreed. "I still remember how strong the blue northers can be."

"They're hard to forget," Margaret agreed.

"What's a 'blue norther'?" Dwylah asked.

"They're cold fronts that come through so fast the temperature can drop fifty degrees or more in an hour. Sometimes there are blizzards with them, too," Penny explained as memories of life on the ranch during the winter returned and she fought down a shiver. "I definitely wouldn't want to be traveling in one."

"Neither would I. I'm cold enough already." Dwylah always liked to sit in front of her fireplace at home when the weather turned bad.

"So you're going to be home in time for Christmas," Margaret said, thinking it would be a happy time for her, and she was surprised by the sudden sadness that showed in the girl's expression.

"Yes," she answered slowly, "I will."

The woman said no more, and they let the conversation lag as they went on to bed. They had to be on the road first thing in the morning, so they needed to get all the rest they could.

In the room where the men were sleeping, Dan lay awake long into the night just staring up at the ceiling. He was satisfied that things had worked out so far. Now he just had to make sure Penny got back safely. He worried that Jack's health might have gotten worse, but he refused to dwell on that. Jack was a tough man, and he was determined to be reunited with his daughter again. Dan knew Jack would be waiting for them when they reached the ranch.

For a moment, Dan found himself thinking of Nick again. He still worried about him and hoped that he'd been happy and had had a better life with the family that had adopted him. He'd missed Nick all these years, and he knew he would never forget him.

Dan closed his eyes and sought sleep.

Tomorrow was going to be a real long day on the trail.

It was after midnight, and Nick lay in bed in his room at the orphanage, unable to sleep. With Miss Lawson's help, all the arrangements had been made, so he could leave on the trip and not have to worry about the home. His thoughts were racing as he imagined seeing his big brother again, and as he thought of Danny, memories of the past overwhelmed him and he knew there was something he had to do—something he hadn't done in years.

Nick got up to light the lamp on his chest of drawers and went to the closet to take out the small trunk he kept stored in the back. He hadn't opened the trunk in a long time, but he knew he had to tonight. With great care, he unlocked it and took out the small, worn Bible. The Bible was the only connection he still had to his family. It had been his mother's, and after she'd died, their father had been so angry he'd thrown it away. Nick had saved it and had kept it hidden from his father. Not that he'd had to hide it for long, for it hadn't been too much later when their father had deserted them at the orphanage and disappeared from their lives forever.

Nick opened the Holy Book now and stared down at the names and birth dates his mother had written on the inside of the back cover. He saw Danny's name there and he prayed that he would find his brother.

Nick closed the Bible and put it carefully back in the trunk. Turning out the lamp, he lay back down, and this time, feeling more at peace, he was able to fall asleep.

Chapter Ten

Nick walked into the lunchroom to join the children for their noon meal. He and Steve were leaving later that afternoon, and he wanted to take this time to tell the children how much he was going to miss them and how they should behave for Miss Lawson while he was gone.

"We're going to miss you, Reverend Miller!" they shouted as he entered the room.

Nick was surprised to find Miss Lawson had arranged for a party for him. She was standing off to the side of the room with Steve watching him in delight. The children all left their seats and came running up to hug him. He was deeply touched by their show of affection. When the children had finally returned to sit at their tables, he went up to the front of the dining room to speak with them.

"As you all know, Steve and I are leaving today for a trip to Texas. Please keep us in your prayers every day. We will be praying for you, too," Nick said.

"When are you coming back?" one of the boys called out. He knew he wasn't supposed to yell that way, but he loved the reverend and was going to miss him real bad while he was gone.

"Right now, I'm not sure," he answered, "but know this—Steve and I are going to miss you, too."

"Christmas won't be the same without you," Miss Lawson told him.

"We'll get back as soon as we can," Nick promised.

They enjoyed the meal together and then after the children were dismissed. He went to speak with Miss Lawson.

"Thank you for everything," he told her.

"You're welcome. Now go find that brother of yours!" she ordered, her eyes lighting up with delight at the thought of their reunion. "You're going to be the best Christmas present your brother Danny ever got, you just wait and see."

Nick smiled tenderly at her. "I feel the same way about him." He looked to Steve, who was standing quietly by his side. "Are you ready to start our trip?"

"Yes, sir."

"Let's go!"

Miss Lawson watched from the doorway as they loaded their luggage into the waiting carriage and climbed in. She was waving to them as they drove away, and she offered up a silent prayer for their safety on their journey—and that they would find his brother.

At first, Penny had found the trip exciting, but as day after day passed and the miles seemed endless, she was beginning to realize what a long, grueling trip it really was. Their conversations had been limited after that first day on the stage because conditions had been crowded ever since.

Dwylah spoke up, jarred to the bone when the stage hit a particular rough spot in the road. "We've only got eight more days to go until we reach Sagebrush, don't we, Dan?"

"If the weather holds," Dan answered. He'd been keeping an eye on the horizon out the stagecoach window, watching for clouds, and it seemed as if the weather was going to stay clear.

"It better hold. I don't want to spend Christmas snowbound in a stagecoach," Dwylah joked, chuckling. "How would Santa ever find us?"

Penny laughed at her friend. "We'll be there long before Christmas. Don't worry."

"I wish we were there already," she said.

"Don't we all?" Lee, one of the three men crammed into the seat across from them in the crowded stagecoach, muttered gruffly.

Lee and his two friends, Carl and Pete, had boarded the stage the day before, and since then he'd been trapped in the crowded coach with the lady who never seemed to stop talking. Of course, he didn't mind being stuck there with the younger woman who was sitting with her. The young woman was one pretty filly. She was easy on the eyes, and though he knew the man sitting with the two women was no doubt traveling with them, it didn't lessen his interest in the sweet-looking one. He kept hoping he could find a way to get a minute or two alone with her at one of the stops during the trip.

Dan was keeping an eye on the rough-looking men who'd boarded the stage the previous day. He'd caught them eyeing Penny with undisguised interest on more than one occasion, and he wasn't about to let them try anything with her. He'd stayed close beside Penny and Dwylah until they retired to the women's quarters the night before, and he planned to do the same tonight. He didn't want any trouble with the other men, but he also wasn't about to let any harm come to the women in his care. Good-looking as she was, he knew Penny would be a temptation to any man, himself included, but he put that thought from him as quickly as it came. He was there to protect her.

"So, where are you ladies heading?" Lee asked.

"Miss Anderson and I are going to her family's ranch in Sagebrush," Dwylah answered in a friendly tone.

"So you're going home," Lee said, giving them a partially toothless grin as he shifted his gaze to the younger woman.

"Yes, it will be good to be with my father again," Penny answered.

"Which ranch is yours?" He could tell she came from money, and he wondered just how rich she really was.

"The Lazy Ace," Dan answered, putting himself in the conversation.

A Cowboy for Christmas

"I've heard it's one of the best around." Lee eyed the Anderson girl with even more interest.

"It is," Dan said.

The knowledge that this little gal was wealthy made her look even better to Lee, and he concentrated harder on figuring out a way to get her alone when they stopped for the night.

When they arrived at the way station, Lee and his rowdy friends were hungry and ate up their dinners real fast, then left to take a look around the stables.

Dwylah finished her meal and was getting ready to settle in for the night. She reached in her pocket to get the small prayer book she always carried with her only to find it was gone. "Oh—"

"What's wrong?" Penny asked, seeing her friend's troubled expression.

"It's my prayer book . . . It must have fallen out of my pocket on the stage. I have to go find it."

"No, you wait here," Dan said, getting up from the table. "I'll go get it for you."

"Why, thank you, Dan," she told him.

Dwylah went on back to the ladies' sleeping room for a moment, leaving Penny alone at the table.

Since it was still light out, Penny went out on the small porch. She knew Dan would be right back and it felt good to be up moving around. She'd been thinking of her father during dinner, and she'd made up her mind that once she got to the ranch, she was going to make his final days as full of happiness as she could. She wanted him to know that she had loved him all this time and had missed him, too.

Dwylah came out to join her there on the porch. "You've been a little quiet tonight."

Penny looked at her traveling companion. "I've been thinking of how much I've missed, being away from my father this long."

"He's going to be so thrilled to see you. I'm sure he's counting the days until you show up, just like we're counting the miles until we get there."

Penny smiled. "It does seem as if we've been traveling for an eternity, but it will all have been worth it once I get to see him again."

"Yes, it will," she agreed. "I'm going to go settle in. Just bring the prayer book on back with you when you come." She was glad that tonight there would only be the two of them sleeping in the women's quarters. The privacy would be wonderful.

"I will." Penny watched her friend go inside, and then, since it wasn't dark yet, she decided to walk back and see if she could find Dan and help him look for the prayer book.

Lee had just started back up to the station from the stable when he saw the pretty little gal who was traveling with them out walking around all by herself. He couldn't believe his luck. He was certain that she'd come out there just looking for him, and he was certainly going to oblige her by going after her.

"Well, howdy, little lady," he said, going straight up to her.

Penny had seen him when she'd first left the porch, but she hadn't paid much attention until he called out to her.

"Hello," she responded, stopping right where she was and wondering what he wanted.

"How you doing tonight?" he asked, his gaze going over her hungrily as he came to stand with her.

Penny saw the look in his eyes and was immediately uncomfortable being alone in his presence. She knew she had to get away from him. She glanced around in hopes of seeing someone else nearby, but right then there was no one around. "I'm fine," she answered. "And I was just going back in."

She turned and started to move away and was shocked when he grabbed her by the arm.

"There's no reason for you to leave just yet, little darling. Why, I'd been hoping I could find a way to get you alone here tonight, and you must have been thinking the same thing."

"Let me go!" Penny tried to pull herself free.

"You don't really want me to let you go, now, do you?" he said, pulling her closer in spite of her resistance.

Penny struggled harder against his hold.

Lee was ready to drag her off behind the stable so he could kiss her when suddenly he heard someone shout.

"Get your hands off her *now*!"

Chapter Eleven

Dan had just found Dwylah's prayer book and had started back to the house when he'd seen Lee go after Penny. He was furious with himself for leaving her alone, but he'd thought she had sense enough to stay with Dwylah inside the station.

"What—" Lee could handle wild women, but this cowboy looked real tough and real mean. "We're just having a little fun here. She came outside looking for me. She was wanting to be with me, ain't that right, honey?" He tightened his grip on her arm threateningly.

"I said, *Let her go.*" Dan's tone was cold and commanding.

Lee was many things, but he wasn't a fool. He finally loosened his grip on the girl.

Penny had never been so glad to see anyone in her whole life as she was to see Dan right then. She ran straight to him and was thrilled when he took her in his arms and held her close. For a moment, she buried her face against his chest as she trembled in relief.

Dan could feel her trembling, and took her by the shoulders and held her back away from him so he could look down at her. "Are you all right?"

"Yes," she said breathlessly.

"He didn't hurt you?" Dan glanced fiercely at the other man, who was backing away, before looking back down at her.

"No, you showed up just in time."

A rush of unexpected emotions jarred him as he gazed at Penny. Her beauty and innocence touched him in a way he'd never experienced before, and a tremor of sensual awareness stirred within him at the feel of her so close to him. Dan called upon his strict self-control to force it away.

"Go back inside with Dwylah," he said. "And here, give this to her." He handed Penny the small prayer book.

"You found it." She took the book from him.

"Yes. Now go."

Still upset over all that had happened, Penny cast one last quick look in the other man's direction. Then without saying another word, she hurried back into the station.

Lee was still standing there, leering at Penny as he watched her go.

"Wipe that look off of your face," Dan snarled. "You don't look at a lady that way."

"So, you're wanting to keep her all for yourself, are you? I saw the way *you* was looking at her." Lee sneered at him. "You just don't want to share her."

His insult to Penny's character infuriated Dan, and Dan covered the distance between them in an instant. Before Lee could even react, Dan hit him and knocked him to the ground. He stood over him, glaring down at him. His tone was as cold as the look in his eyes when he told him, "Miss Anderson is a lady. Remember that. Don't ever go near her or talk about her again. Do you understand me?"

Lee was quaking as he wiped the blood from his lip. Angry as the man seemed to be, Lee was afraid he might go for his gun, and he was real relieved when he didn't. "Yeah."

"What?" Dan demanded.

"I understand you."

Dan gave him one last threatening look and started to turn away to go check on Penny. It was then that he saw the driver and the man riding shotgun come out of the stable with the man's two friends to see what was going on. After Dan had given an account of the situation, the driver pronounced: "You and your friends won't be riding out with us in the morning."

"What?" Pete snarled, stepping up to the driver.

"We've got ladies on this run," the driver said, "and we don't need men like your friend, here, causing trouble for them."

"We paid our fares!" Lee argued.

"Yes, you did, and that's why I'm letting you wait here at the station for the next stage that's coming through. There will be one the day after tomorrow," the driver dictated.

The three men wanted to argue, but they knew there was no use.

"All right." Lee gave in. Both the driver and the man riding shotgun looked real mean, and though he and Pete and Carl were always ready for a good fight, he didn't see any point in trying to take them. One more night at the way station wouldn't matter.

"And listen up!" the driver continued. "I don't want you anywhere near the women. You and your friends will be sleeping out in the stable tonight."

"Yeah," he replied again.

Again, Pete and Carl glared at their friend but said nothing. It wasn't unusual for Lee to get himself in trouble.

Dan was satisfied with the way the driver had handled things. He left them to go check on Penny and found her in the main room with Dwylah, the stationmaster, and his wife.

Knowing they needed a moment alone, the stationmaster and his wife went out to talk to the driver and find out all that had happened.

"The driver's taken care of things." Dan explained to Penny and Dwylah what the driver had ordered the three men to do.

"That's good. That's real good. Thank you, Dan," Dwylah declared, very proud of him.

Dan looked to Penny once more. Why, if anything had happened to her, he would never have forgiven himself. "From the way things are going, I'm not going to be able to let you out of my sight even for a few minutes. I told you to wait inside."

Penny was a little shocked by the fierceness of his tone. "I'm sorry."

He went on, "From now on, I may just have to tie you up and keep you with me all the time."

Dwylah stood silently back, watching the interaction between them with more than a little interest and fighting down a smile.

The stationmaster came inside then. "I'm glad you weren't injured, Miss Anderson. Sometimes the boys on these runs can get a little wild, but it's all taken care of now."

Dwylah spoke up. "Yes, it is, and I think it's time for us to call it a night."

"I think you're right," Penny agreed. She looked up at Dan once more, trying to judge his mood. His expression was closely guarded, though, so she couldn't really tell what he was thinking. In that moment, she almost felt as if he were her guardian angel. He had been there to save her when she'd been in trouble. She didn't even want to think about what might have happened if he hadn't come to help her when he did. She reached out to gently touch his arm, and in that simple touch she could feel the strength of him. "Dan, thank you."

Dan nodded, all too aware of her hand on his arm.

Dwylah wasn't about to let him off that easily. When Penny moved away, she went after him.

"Come here, you," she declared, grabbing Dan by the arm.

Her move surprised him, and he frowned slightly as he looked down at her, wondering what was troubling her. "What's wrong?"

"Nothing's wrong." She kept her hold on his arm and pulled him down to her so she could kiss his cheek. "You're my hero, Danny."

It was the first time anyone had called him Danny in years, and it touched something deep within him, hearing it from her. He couldn't help himself; even as serious as he was right then, he found himself smiling down at her. "I was just doing my job, ma'am."

Dwylah's heart swooned at the change in him when he smiled. She'd always thought he was handsome, but he had always been so serious. Now, when he smiled at her—why, she thought he was downright breathtaking. "Oh, you! Good night."

"Good night," he told them, and he kept watch until they were safely in the back room with the door locked.

It was a short time later as Penny and Dwylah were getting ready for bed that Dwylah brought up the topic she'd been pondering for some time now.

"I've been thinking . . ." Dwylah began.

She sounded so serious, Penny grew curious. "What about?"

"About how lucky you are."

"I am?"

"Oh yes. Didn't you hear Danny? He said he wasn't going to take his eyes off of you. He said he might even tie you up and keep you with him all the time from now on," she finished with an impish grin. "You would definitely be one lucky lady if he decided to do that."

"Oh, Dwylah!" Penny couldn't help it. She started laughing with her outrageous friend.

"You know, he is so sweet—and so handsome. I was just wondering if I could convince the stage driver to take us to the nearest justice of the peace, so I could get him to marry me before somebody else snatches him up."

"A woman could do a lot worse," Penny told her, remembering what it had felt like to be in his arms.

Both women were smiling as they went to bed.

As Penny lay curled on her side on the hard cot, the memory of the whole scene with the man named Lee returned. A shiver of disgust went through her at the thought of his hands upon her, and in the same moment, she remembered how she'd felt when Dan had drawn her to him. A distant memory of dancing with Richard at the ball returned, and Penny realized being in Dan's arms had been far more exciting than being in Richard's. She was wondering what it would be like to dance with Dan—or even to kiss him—as she drifted off to sleep.

* * *

And she was in Dan's thoughts as he lay awake on his cot in the back room. He was still angry with himself over what had almost happened to her that evening. He hadn't really let his guard down, but he knew he would have to be even more vigilant on the rest of the journey. He couldn't let any harm come to her.

For a moment, Dan remembered how it had felt to hold Penny close and he fought back a groan as he rolled over, seeking sleep. He knew he wouldn't get any rest at all if he kept thinking about Penny.

At dawn, everyone was up and moving.

"The weather's clear and cold today," the driver remarked when he pulled the stage up in front of the way station and jumped down to help load up the luggage. "We should make some real good time."

"That's good news. The sooner we get to Sagebrush, the better," Dan said as he came out of the station with the women. He caught sight of Lee standing near the stable and gave him a look that sent him scurrying back into the stable. After helping the women into the stage, Dan climbed in, too, and sat down opposite them.

"All right," Dwylah began. "Now is the perfect time."

"The perfect time for what?" Dan asked, sensing she was up to something.

"It's the perfect time for you to tell us some of your stories about the Wild West! I need to learn all I can about ranching before we get to the Lazy Ace."

"So you're planning on staying on at the ranch?"

"For as long as Penny needs me," she affirmed. "Now—what's the most exciting thing that's happened to you?"

"Well, there was the time when I was working for another spread and there was an Indian raid—"

"Indians?" Dwylah's eyes widened with interest. "Tell me everything!"

And he did—within reason.

Chapter Twelve

Six days later

Lacey McCormick was desperate. In her life, when things got bad, they usually always got worse, and now it had happened again.

Here she was, walking along the dusty road, wearing a thin coat over her red satin working dress from the Midnight Saloon, and her riding boots. Lacey was thankful that she'd been able to escape the saloon last night and get this good head start. Otherwise Phil, the saloon owner, might have caught up with her already.

At the thought that Phil might be coming after her, Lacey glanced quickly back the way she'd come. She was relieved there was no sign of anyone behind her as far as she could see. She didn't really know if he would try to track her down or not, but she wasn't going to take any chances or let her guard down—not yet.

Lacey had told Phil when she'd started working for him that she wouldn't do anything more than wait tables. He had been satisfied with her work for quite a while, but when some of the ranch hands started to offer him a lot of money for the chance to get her upstairs, Phil had changed. He had tried to convince her to start really "working" at the saloon, but she'd refused and had threatened to quit. Then last night, one of the other saloon girls had warned her that she'd heard some of the wilder boys planning to get her upstairs that very evening, and in that moment, she'd realized she had no choice.

She had to get out of there—

She had to run.

So Lacey had gotten her horse and had ridden out of town before any of them had noticed she was missing. She'd ridden all night and had been making good time until midmorning, when her horse had gone lame. She'd turned the horse loose, and now was alone and on foot, carrying her canteen with her. She kept hoping she might run into someone who could help her, but with the way her life had gone so far, she was reasonably certain that wasn't going to happen.

It was up to her to save herself.

She just had to keep moving.

Lacey thought about praying for help, but wondered if it would do any good. She'd been praying for a miracle in her life for a long time, and look where it had gotten her—she was alone in the middle of nowhere with only a few dollars to her name. Even so, she offered up a silent prayer for help and guidance.

She started to cry, but finally with an effort, she forced her weaker emotions away. She had to be strong right now. She couldn't give up. She still remembered her grandma telling her when she'd been a little girl that life was all about surviving, and she knew that's what she had to do now.

Lacey kept moving down the rocky road. If nothing else, she hoped she might find a way station where she could stay until the next stagecoach came through. That one thought kept her going.

Nick sat next to Steve on the stagecoach, watching the boy as he all but hung out the window staring at the passing landscape. Even after all these days of traveling, Steve was still excited to get up every morning and get on the road again. Nick knew he'd done the right thing bringing him along. This trip was an adventure for him and one he would remember his whole life.

Nick also knew Steve wouldn't be the only one remembering this trip. Just the thought of possibly being reunited with Danny again lifted his spirits and excited him, too. He realized there was a good chance Danny wouldn't be in Sagebrush when they finally got there, but he tried not to think about that right now. One way or another, he was going to track his brother down. He'd come this far and he wasn't going to give up. He couldn't wait to see Danny's expression when they faced each other for the first time. The thought alone made him smile.

"You thinkin' about your brother?" Steve asked as he glanced back at Reverend Miller.

"Yes, how did you know?"

"You're smilin'," he answered simply.

"It could be I'm just having fun," Nick teased him.

"Are you?"

"Yes. This is one exciting trip for me."

"Me, too," Steve said. He knew he would always be grateful to Reverend Miller for bringing him along.

There was a middle-aged married couple sitting across from them, and the woman remarked with more than a little disbelief, "You both think this trip is exciting?"

"Yes, ma'am," Steve answered. "Reverend Miller's going to see his brother again."

"Oh, you're not his son?" she asked in surprise, looking between them.

Her question surprised and touched Steve. He looked up at the reverend as he answered, "No, ma'am. I'm an orphan and Reverend Miller takes care of me at the Children's Home in St. Louis."

She looked at the young preacher with even more respect. "That's quite a calling you have, Reverend Miller."

"Yes, ma'am, it is," he agreed, smiling at Steve. "I've been very blessed to work with the children, especially Steve."

"And it seems the children have been blessed to have you," she replied. "We're the Wilsons, by the way."

"It's nice to meet you."

"You, too."

They fell into an easy silence for a while, and Steve eventually nodded off, nestled against Nick's side. Nick looked down at the sleeping boy and knew how special he truly was. He certainly could sympathize with what Steve was going through. He understood all his troubled emotions, having suffered the same fate all those years ago when he and Danny had been left at the orphanage. It was that memory that had made him determined to be there for Steve and the other children, in good times and in bad. The thought that the lady traveling with them believed Steve was his son had touched him deeply. Nick would have been proud to claim him as his own.

It was over an hour later when they were all startled by the stagecoach coming to a sudden, abrupt halt.

"What is it, dear?" Mrs. Wilson asked. "We're not getting robbed, are we?"

Her husband took a quick look out the stage window. "I don't see anything . . ." He leaned farther out and yelled, "Driver! What's wrong?"

"Take it easy, folks. It's nothing to worry about," the driver called back. They heard him jump down from his bench.

"Wait here, Steve," Nick said. "There might be something blocking the road. I'll go see if I can help him."

"I could help, too," Steve was quick to offer.

"Let me make sure it's safe, first."

"Yes, sir." The boy nodded obediently and sat back.

Nick got out of the stage and went up to see what was going on. He'd expected it to be something simple from the way the driver had talked, and he was shocked by what he discovered. The driver was standing in the road, talking with a beautiful, young, blonde-haired woman. Nick frowned, wondering how in the world she'd come to be in the middle of nowhere on foot, and then his expression darkened even more as he realized the girl was wearing a light coat over a rather short red dress that showed a length of her legs and a pair of riding boots. His instincts told him she was in trouble, and he knew they couldn't just leave her there on her own.

"I appreciate you stopping. My horse went lame some miles back and I've been on foot ever since. I've got some money. I can pay you fifty cents if you'll take me with you. I'll even ride up on top if there's no room in the stage."

"You need any help, Jim?" Nick asked as he moved forward.

Lacey had been so desperately trying to convince the driver to take her along that she hadn't heard the other man get out of the stage, and she was startled by his presence. She was used to dealing with men like the driver and the hard-drinking cowhands, and her eyes widened a bit at the sight of the handsome stranger coming their way. He looked to be quite a gentleman.

"Our little missy here does," the driver replied. He looked to the girl again and said, "Climb on up with me."

Nick understood what the driver was doing, but he quickly interceded. "There's room in the stage. She can ride with us. It'll be warmer in there."

"You sure?"

"Yes," Nick answered without hesitation.

"All right, come on," the driver told her. "Let's get you in the stage. I'm already behind schedule."

"Do you want me to pay you now?"

"Later. Let's go," he urged, ushering her back to the stagecoach door.

Lacey was completely surprised when the other man held the stage door for her and took her elbow to help her in. A shiver of awareness went through her at his simple touch and she paused to look up at him. The moment left her breathless when she saw the true look of gentleness and kindness in his dark eyes. "Thank you."

"What is going on?" Mr. Wilson demanded of the driver as he watched the girl climb in.

"This young lady was stranded out here and needs a ride, so she'll be traveling with us," he explained.

"You were stranded? Out here?" Mrs. Wilson shifted closer to her husband, casting a disdainful eye over their new companion.

Lacey had dealt with folks like them before.

She said nothing, trying to scoot as far away from the woman as she could on the seat.

Nick got in after her and sat back down beside Steve. He took one look at Mrs. Wilson's expression and offered to the new girl, "There's more room on this side, if you don't mind sitting with us."

"Why, thanks. I don't mind at all." Lacey didn't hesitate to switch. She certainly had no objection to sitting next to him, and she could just imagine how awkward the ride would have been if she'd had to try to keep a distance between her and the older woman.

Steve smiled at the new lady. "Hi, I'm Steve. What's your name?"

Lacey was surprised the boy talked to her, especially after the way the couple had reacted to her presence. She smiled warmly at him. "My name's Lacey. It's nice to meet you, Steve."

"It's nice to meet you, too. This is Reverend Miller. We're going to Sagebrush, Texas. Where are you going?"

Lacey looked quickly at the handsome man beside her, startled by the news that he was a minister, but then she realized she had sensed something special about him. "Hello, Reverend."

"Lacey," he returned.

Knowing he was a man of God, she felt uncomfortable now with her first thoughts about him. "Why, I'm heading toward Sagebrush, too." Lacey told herself it wasn't a lie. She was on the same stagecoach they were. "I'm just glad you came along when you did. My horse went lame and I've been walking for quite a while."

Nick couldn't even imagine how she'd ended up where she was, but he knew he was glad that they'd happened upon her. There was no telling what danger she might have encountered all alone out in the middle of nowhere. "We're glad we did, too."

Lacey was touched by his kind words and smiled a little timidly at him. She remembered her earlier prayer for help and knew it had been answered. She didn't know where she was going from here or where she'd end up, but, at least for the time being, she was safe.

They all fell silent as the stage traveled on. They still had a long way to go until they stopped for the night.

Nick hadn't found himself in a situation like this one before, but he had a feeling there might be a little trouble when they did stop at the way station. The girl named Lacey had brought no luggage with her, so she had only the clothes she was wearing, and he knew it wouldn't be appropriate for Steve to see a lady dressed in such a manner. As long as Lacey kept her coat on, there wouldn't be a problem, but once they stopped to eat and bed down for the night, he wasn't sure what would happen. Determined to protect Steve, he made up his mind to take Lacey aside when they stopped and offer her a change of clothing. He had an extra shirt he could give her, but he didn't know what to do about anything else. He could give her a pair of his pants, too, but he knew they would be far too big for her. With her boots, the pants would work, if they could find a length of rope to use for a belt—if she was willing. One way or the other, he would soon find out.

It was just about dark when the stage pulled to a stop at the station. The Wilsons got out first, and then Nick climbed down. He waited while Steve got out and then offered Lacey a hand to help her descend. For a moment as she stepped down, Nick got a clear view of her lovely legs, and he had to force his gaze away.

"Thank you, Reverend," Lacey said, smiling up at him.

Nick looked over to see that Steve had already gone into the station. "Lacey, I was wondering if I could speak with you for a moment."

She glanced at him, a little unsure. "What about?"

"Steve."

"The boy?"

"Yes." Nick didn't pause as he continued. "I saw that you didn't have any luggage with you, and I couldn't help noticing that the gown you're wearing is . . . well . . ."

"Fit for a saloon girl," she finished for him.

"Yes, and Steve's still a young boy, and I don't think it would be appropriate for him to see you dressed this way."

"You don't have to worry, preacher man," she replied, her tone curt. "I'll keep my coat on." She was humiliated, but she understood what he meant. The boy seemed sweet and innocent, and she wanted him to stay that way. She started to turn away.

Nick saw her reaction and felt bad. He hadn't meant for her to be insulted. He'd just wanted to help. Instinctively, he caught her by the arm before she could walk away. "Wait, that isn't what I meant."

She looked from his hand on her arm up to his face, her expression challenging, and Nick quickly dropped his hand from her.

"What I wanted to do, since you obviously don't have a change of clothes, was to offer you something else more comfortable to wear. I've got an extra shirt and an extra pair of pants. I'm sure they'll be too big for you, but they might be more comfortable for riding on the stage."

Lacey had rarely had anyone take care of her. She told herself he was a man of God, but still, she didn't trust him, or anyone else for that matter. Her eyes narrowed as she demanded of him, "What do you want from me?"

Nick was shocked by her reaction to his offer and his expression showed it. "Why, nothing— nothing at all. I just thought you needed some help and I wanted to do what I could for you. As children of God we're supposed to help each other in times of need."

Lacey was used to men leering at her, and she was completely taken aback by his response. She realized then he truly was acting out of kindness and generosity. "Thank you, Reverend Miller. I appreciate your offer, and, yes, you're right. I do need a change of clothes."

"I'll get them for you as soon as they bring our bags inside." Nick gave her a gentle smile and followed her into the station.

Mindful of Reverend Miller's concerns about little Steve, she kept her coat on, even though it was comfortably warm inside. It wasn't long before the other travelers' bags were brought in.

Nick took his bag back into the men's sleeping room and took out a pair of black pants and a white shirt. As slender as she was, he wished he'd had an extra belt to give her, but he had a feeling she was resourceful enough to think of some way to keep the pants on.

"What are you doing?" Steve asked, having followed him into the room.

"I thought our new friend might be a little cold, so I was going to give her some warmer clothes to wear."

"You want me to take them to her?" he offered.

"Sure," Nick replied. He gave Steve the clothes and then followed him back out into the main room. He watched as the boy hurried over to where Lacey was standing all by herself.

"Here!" Steve said. "Reverend Miller said these are for you!"

"Why, thank you, Steve." Lacey took the offered clothing and looked across the room to see the preacher standing there watching her. "And you, too, Reverend."

"You're welcome," Steve said proudly. "Are you gonna put them on now, so you'll stay warm?"

"Yes, I am," she told him. "I'll be right back."

Lacey knew the married couple was watching her, so she hurried off into the room she'd been told was the women's sleeping room, and she shut the door. She took off her coat and quickly shed the red dress. As she threw it down on one of the cots, she knew she never wanted to wear it again. She took off her socks and her boots and unlaced her corset. As big and baggy as the preacher's clothes were going to be on her, she didn't see the need to wear it any longer. She stripped off her garters and stockings, and then pulled on the pants. They were way too large for her. In fact, she knew they wouldn't stay up unless she could figure out something to use as a belt. She took one look at her garters and quickly fastened them together. A makeshift belt was better than none, and she was right. It was tight enough to keep the pants from slipping down. Lacey donned the shirt. It, too, was far too big, but she didn't care. She tucked it into the waist of the pants and then put on her socks and boots again.

Lacey had just started from the room when she caught sight of her own reflection in the small mirror over the washstand. She stopped to stare at herself. The Lacey who'd worked at the saloon had disappeared. The girl looking back at her with her hair straggling down, wearing men's clothes, looked like a total stranger.

Only then did she realize just how dirty she was from all the riding and walking she'd done. She went to the washstand, rolled up the shirt-sleeves, and quickly scrubbed her face and arms clean. She longed for a real bath or even a brush to tend to her hair, but she knew that wasn't going to happen. Instead, she tore a small piece of ribbon off her dress and used it to tie her hair back.

Lacey took one last quick look in the mirror and knew this was as good as it was going to get. She smiled at the thought that if she cut her hair off, she might even pass for a boy, dressed in the baggy clothes she was wearing. She doubted Phil would even have been able to recognize her then, not that he would chase after her this far, but it did make her feel better knowing she would never have to go back to working for him again. Somehow, she would survive. Lacey got her small change purse out of her coat pocket and put it in her pants pocket before going back out into the main room. She had to keep it with her. She couldn't risk losing what little money she had.

"Oh—" Mrs. Wilson looked shocked at Lacey's attire as she came back into the main room.

Lacey had expected the other woman to react this way, and she slanted her an easy smile. "These clothes are definitely warmer than what I was wearing. Thank you, Reverend Miller."

The Wilsons went to sit in two chairs before the fireplace so they could ignore the others.

Steve and Nick were seated at the main table and they both looked over at Lacey and smiled.

"You look like a boy!" Steve laughed in his innocent way.

"I know," she returned, laughing, too, as she went to join them at the table. She sat across from the reverend, next to the boy.

"I'm glad the clothes worked out for you."

"So am I."

Right then the stage driver came in.

"Well, ain't that a change!" he said, catching sight of her dressed that way for the first time. "All right, girly, I need some money from you now. Nobody gets a free ride on my stage."

"I know," Lacey replied. She got up from the table and went to talk with him quietly. She didn't want anyone to know how desperate she was. "How much is it to Sagebrush?"

He quoted her the price, and she knew she wasn't going to Sagebrush.

"How far can I get on twenty-five cents?" she asked.

As quiet as she was trying to be, Nick and Steve could still hear their conversation. Steve looked up at him, his expression anxious after he realized just how poor she was.

"We gotta help her," Steve said in a low voice, urging him on.

Nick didn't say anything, he just got up and went to join the conversation. "Steve and I will cover her fare for the rest of the trip to Sagebrush."

The driver was surprised. "Are you sure, Reverend?"

"Yes."

The driver told him the cost of her fare, and Nick paid him.

"All right," the driver said. "You're going to Sagebrush."

Lacey went back to sit at the table with Steve.

"Reverend Miller takes care of everything," Steve said with confidence.

"So I'm finding out," she replied. Once the reverend sat down across from them again, she offered, "I'm going to pay you back. Take what I've got here and—"

"Don't even think about it," he said.

"I don't like owing people."

"You don't owe me anything."

"But—"

Nick cut her off. "Consider it an early Christmas present."

Humbled, Lacey looked up at him, knowing she'd never met anyone like the reverend and Steve before.

"Thank you," she said quietly, and she meant it.

Chapter Thirteen

Penny stared out the window at the now vaguely familiar Texas landscape and knew their long trip would soon be over. She was almost home—with her father. The driver had told them when they'd started out that morning that they would make it to Sagebrush that very day, and she couldn't wait.

As excited as she was, though, her mood was torn between the thrill of finally being back and uneasiness over what kind of reception she was going to get from her father. He obviously wanted her with him or he wouldn't have sent Dan all the way to St. Louis to get her, but she couldn't help wondering, as the moment of their reunion drew near, what he would think of her. She certainly knew how she'd felt when she'd never heard from him for so long, and she was sure he believed the same about her—that she didn't love him or care about him. Starting this afternoon when they were reunited she was going to make every effort to convince him that she had nothing to do with her mother's and her aunt's deception. She just hoped he would believe her.

"Penny, are you all right?" Dwylah asked when

she noticed how quiet she had become and how serious her expression was.

"Yes, I'm fine. I was just thinking about my father. It's been so long. Do you think he'll be in town to meet us, Dan?"

"I don't know. I sent the wire to let them know when we'd be arriving, so it will probably depend on how he's feeling."

"I hope he's there."

"So do I," he agreed.

It was midafternoon when the stage made its way down the main street of Sagebrush to the stage office to drop off the passengers and see about picking up new ones. When they came to a halt in front of the office, the driver jumped down and opened the door for them. Dan climbed out first, while the driver and the man riding shotgun went to unload their bags.

"We're here," Dan said as he helped Penny and Dwylah down from the stage.

Penny looked quickly around, hoping to find her father there waiting for her. She was sure she would still recognize him even after all this time, but she saw no sign of him anywhere and her spirits fell.

A man came out of the stage office just then to greet them.

"Good to see you made it back, Dan." He went to shake Dan's hand.

"Finally," Dan replied.

The man looked to the two women with Dan and quickly introduced himself. "I'm Ben Harper, the clerk here in Sagebrush. I take it you're Miss Anderson?"

"Yes, I'm Penny Anderson, and this is Miss Carpenter, my traveling companion and chaperone."

"Well, Miss Anderson, it's nice to meet you. You, too, Miss Carpenter. Looks like Dan did a fine job getting you here."

"Yes, he did," Dwylah agreed.

"Is Jack in town, Ben?" Dan asked.

"No. One of the hands came in earlier by himself to wait for you to show up. Why don't you come on in the office while I send for him?"

"Thank you." Penny and Dwylah started to follow him, leaving their bags outside.

"You don't have to send for him. I'll go find him," Dan offered as he held the office door open for them. He knew Lou was probably the one who'd come to pick them up, and he knew right where his friend would be biding his time, waiting for the stage to pull in. "I'll be right back."

Penny sat down next to Dwylah on the small bench near the office door to await Dan's return.

"Are you all right, dear?" Dwylah asked, seeing the look of sadness in the young woman's eyes. She had thought Penny would be excited when they finally arrived in town.

"It's my father. I know he's ill, but I was hoping he would be here."

"I understand," she sympathized, knowing she was finally going to have to face the reality of her father's weakened and deteriorating condition. "Is it a long ride out to the ranch?"

"About half an hour."

"If he's as ill as Dan said he was, he's probably better off staying on the ranch waiting for you there to save his strength."

"I know." Penny sighed and looked out the window at the main street of the town. Wanting to distract herself for a moment, she added, "Sagebrush has grown since I've been away."

"Really?" Dwylah was surprised. There didn't seem to be much to this "town" now, so she could only imagine what it had been like when her mother had taken her away all those years ago.

"It was only about half this size when we left."

"Are you looking forward to staying here permanently?"

"I think so."

"It's going to be a hard decision for you, I know, so I'll stay on with you for as long as you want me to."

She was thankful for the offer and her mood lightened a bit as she teased her, "Forever?"

Dwylah teased back, "You never know. If I can get Danny to go find the justice of the peace with me, I won't be going anywhere—at least, I wouldn't be going anywhere without him!" She got a smile out of Penny, and that was what she'd been hoping for. She patted her hand affectionately. "You'll be back with your father very soon now. This is the day you've been waiting for, for so long, and it's finally here."

Penny lifted her hopeful gaze to hers. "Yes, it is."

"You want another whiskey, Lou?" Mike, the bartender, asked as he came back, bottle in hand, to where the ranch hand from the Lazy Ace was standing at the bar.

"No, I'm just having the one today," Lou said as he pushed his empty glass back across to him. "I've got to be ready to leave for the ranch as soon as Dan shows up with the girl."

"You're a strong-willed man, Lou," Mike told him with a chuckle. "It isn't often I get turned down on a refill."

"Some days I am, but not always," Lou said, but he wasn't laughing. There wasn't much right now to laugh about. "Ben said he didn't know if the stage was going to be on time or not today."

"He's right. You never know when it's going to pull in. There are days when we're lucky if they get here at all."

"Let's hope this isn't one of those days. Jack's been waiting for this moment for a real long time."

"How's he been holding up?" Mike had heard

the talk around town about the rancher being sick and his daughter coming back.

"It's hit him real hard. He's used to being strong, and it doesn't suit him to be this weak and to have to rely on others."

"Then it's good his girl is coming back. I remember when Jack's wife took off with her. Jack loved that little girl, but times were harder back then and, I guess, his wife had had enough."

They got no chance to say any more, for right then Dan came walking into the saloon.

"Well, look who's here!" Mike said.

"Dan! Good to see you," Lou greeted him.

"We just got here. The women are waiting for us down at the stage office. How have things been going?" he asked, coming to join Lou at the bar. He wanted to hear the worst of Jack's condition away from the women.

"He's about the same as when you left. He doesn't get out of the house much, but he is still up and moving."

Dan was relieved to hear it. "Good. I've been worrying about him."

"Let's get the carriage and go home. I think he might be real glad to see you, what do you think?"

"I think you're right, and I'm going to be real glad to see him."

"How's his little girl?"

"She's not a 'little girl' anymore," Dan told him.

"All grown up, is she?"

"That she is," Dan declared.

As soon as Penny heard the carriage pull up in front of the stage office, she was out the door and ready to go, eager to be reunited with her father at last.

"Lou?" Penny couldn't believe it when she found herself face-to-face with one of her favorite ranch hands from her childhood. Unable to resist, she ran straight to him and gave him a hug.

Lou hadn't been sure what to expect, but the moment he saw her, he recognized her. He returned her hug and then held her back to get a good look at her. "Penny, gal, you are all grown up, just like Dan told me."

"It's so good to see you," she told him, smiling up at him, and then she quickly introduced him to Dwylah.

"It's nice to meet you." Lou tipped his hat to the older woman. "Thanks for taking such good care of our little Penny here."

"It wasn't easy. She's a wild one, that girl, but Danny and I managed," she told him.

Dan had just finished putting the last bag in the back of the carriage. "Looks like we're ready to go."

"Tell Jack I said hello," Ben offered as he watched them get ready to leave.

"I will," Dan promised. He turned back to help the women into the carriage before climbing up to sit with Lou for the ride back.

"Be sure to hold on as best you can," Lou advised the women. "The road's a rough one."

"See you later," Ben bid them.

"Thanks for your help, Ben." Lou urged the team on.

Penny and Dwylah shared a knowing look as they began the last part of her journey home.

"I'm almost there—" Penny said softly to Dwylah.

The older woman patted her hand gently. "It won't be long now."

Penny said no more as she prepared herself for the upcoming reunion with her father. Her mother had always told her that he'd been furious with them for leaving, and that was why her mother had never, ever considered returning even for a visit. Somehow, Penelope knew there had to have been more to the separation than that, especially since she'd learned the truth about her father's attempts to stay in touch with her. Before the day was over, she planned to set things right between them.

"So, Lou, how long have you been working on the ranch?" Dwylah asked.

"Some days it feels like I've been working here too long," Lou chuckled. "But I guess I've been riding the Lazy Ace brand for about eight years now."

"And you like it?"

"There are always good times and bad times, but there's nothing else I'd rather be doing, and no other boss I'd want to be working for. Jack Anderson is a good man. He's worked hard, and he's turned the Lazy Ace into a real fine spread."

"So it's a quiet life out here?" Dwylah asked. "We hear so much about the 'Wild West,' and I've read quite a few of the dime novels. Everything seems so violent."

Lou glanced at Dan and answered, "There are hard times. I can't deny that, but you make the best of it. Why, I still remember the time when things got rough back when Hank was the foreman—"

Penny spoke up, vaguely remembering the other man who'd been the foreman when she'd left. "What happened then?"

Lou shared a quick look with Dan as he realized for the first time that she didn't know what had gone on there. "It's a long story, but Hank had been causing a lot of trouble with his drinking, so your daddy fired him. Hank wasn't too happy about that, so he was planning on getting even. Jack's always said it was a real good thing Dan was in the saloon in town that night."

Penny looked at Dan in surprise. "What happened?"

Lou went on to tell her about her father's confrontation with the drunken Hank and how Dan had stepped in.

"It was a good thing you were in the saloon that night," Penny agreed.

"So you like jumping into fights that aren't your own?" Dwylah asked, giving Dan a grin. Her respect for him was growing even more, if that was possible.

"Sometimes a man has to do crazy things," Dan told her.

"I'm glad you did," Penny said. She didn't even want to think about how things might have turned out if he hadn't been there.

They fell silent for a while. When they topped a low rise that overlooked the valley below, Lou stopped the carriage.

"You're home, Penny," Lou said.

Penny looked down in the valley to see the house. Tears blurred her vision as she remembered all the loving, beautiful times they'd shared there—when they'd been a real family.

"What a nice house," Dwylah said, impressed by the large two-story home and multiple outbuildings. On the trip there, she'd tried not to think about what the ranch house would be like. Whenever she'd heard Penny's mother talk about it, she'd always said how crude and uncivilized life was there. Yet here before her was a house that looked spacious and well maintained. It certainly was no run-down, one-room shanty, as everyone who'd listened to her had been led to believe.

"It is lovely—" Penny said softly, staring out across the land.

"How much of the land is yours?" Dwylah asked.

Dan answered her, "As far as you can see, it's all the Lazy Ace."

"Let's go home," Penny told Lou.

Lou started the team up again and they covered the final miles to the ranch house.

Chapter Fourteen

Physically, Jack was feeling weak, and his emotions were in turmoil as he sat on the sofa in the parlor—waiting.

Soon, very soon, his little Penny would be coming through the front door.

Jack wasn't quite sure what to expect. He didn't know how she was feeling about returning to the ranch, but he hoped their reunion would be a good one and they would be able to heal things between them. He needed that peace before he could leave this world, and he needed to know, too, that the Lazy Ace was safe in her hands. As a young girl, she had enjoyed ranch life, and though he'd rarely heard from her since her mother had taken her away, he was hoping she would be interested in staying on. The ranch was his life's work, and he wanted her to cherish it as much as he did.

At the sound of the carriage pulling up outside, Jack mustered what strength he could and got to his feet. He made his way to the doorway at the front hall.

Penny didn't wait for Dan or Lou to come help her from the carriage. The minute the horses came to a stop, she jumped down and ran up to the house. She didn't know what to expect from her homecoming, but she was here—and somewhere inside the house, her father was waiting for her.

Penny dashed up the steps to the porch. Memories from her childhood swept over her as she let herself in, and instinctively as she'd always done as a child, she called out, "Papa, I'm home!"

And it was then she saw him, standing in the parlor doorway.

"Papa—" She had so much to say, so much to tell him, but in that moment, she was silent. Her memories of her big strong father were clear, and she saw the change in him right away. He looked older now, and it seemed as if the life in him was draining away.

Jack stared at Penny, seeing what a lovely young woman she'd grown into. He had missed her so much and now, to have her finally here with him . . .

She took a tentative step toward him and was thrilled when he opened his arms to her. Without hesitation, she went into his welcoming embrace.

"Penny, you're home!" Jack said, wrapping his arms around her and holding her near. "My little girl's finally come home."

"Oh, Papa!" Penny's tears fell freely as she treasured this moment of closeness. She had forgotten over the years how safe and protected she'd always felt when he'd hugged her.

"It's been so long." Jack drew back and looked down at her. "You've grown up, and you're so beautiful."

She managed a teary smile at his words. "And you're just as handsome as I remembered."

He chuckled at her teasing and slipped an arm about her shoulders to hold her close to his side as he turned to greet the woman who'd just followed her into the house with Dan. "Welcome to the Lazy Ace. I'm Jack Anderson, and you must be the chaperone."

"I am," Dwylah replied, and she quickly introduced herself. She was thrilled to see him and Penny together. She had been worried about what condition they would find him in upon their arrival, and she was relieved he was strong enough to be up and around—and that he had hugged his daughter. "It's a pleasure to meet you, sir, and I must tell you, you have a wonderful daughter."

"I know." Jack gazed down at Penny to find she was smiling up at him. "How was the trip?"

"Long," Penny answered. "I thought we were never going to get here, but thank heaven the weather was good so there were no delays."

"You didn't run into any trouble along the way?" he asked. He'd been worried about the danger of the trip, and that was why he'd sent Dan to accompany her.

"Nothing Dan couldn't handle," Penny answered.

"Good." Jack could feel his strength waning. "Come on, let's go in the parlor."

Dan was glad their reunion seemed to be going well. "Jack, where do you want me to put their bags?"

"Take them on upstairs, Dan. Penny's room is at the far end of the hall and Miss Dwylah will be using the bedroom to the right at the top of the stairs," he directed.

"I get to stay in my old bedroom?" Penny was delighted at the news.

"It's yours, isn't it?" he replied.

Jack led the way into the parlor.

Dan was feeling real good as he went upstairs with the first load of bags. He hadn't seen Jack looking this happy in a long time. He felt a great sense of satisfaction that their reunion seemed to be going well. They had a lot to catch up on and to set straight between them, but the hard part was over—Penny was home.

Dan put Dwylah's bags in her room, then went back out to the carriage to get Penny's luggage. Returning upstairs, he made his way down the hall to the room Jack had said was hers. He opened the door and was surprised by what he found. The room looked like it belonged to a child, and he realized then that Jack hadn't changed it in all the years she'd been away. Dan knew it was going to be a surprise for Penny when she finally came upstairs to find everything probably very much the way it had been when she left. He put her bags in her room and went back downstairs.

"Jack, is there anything else I can do for you?" Dan asked as he stood in the parlor doorway.

"You've already done plenty. Thanks for your help," Jack told him as he sat comfortably on the sofa with Penny next to him and Dwylah in the armchair facing them.

Dan left the house, ready to get back to his normal routine. The other ranch hands had watched them ride in, so he figured they'd have a lot of questions for him when he joined Lou down at the stable, and he was right.

"What's she like now?" Fred asked as he and several of the other men cornered Dan.

"She's a lady," he answered.

"Is she as pretty as her mother was?"

"I never met her mother, but from the portrait Jack's got, I'd say she's even prettier," Dan told him.

"Well, that'll liven things up around here," one of the newer ranch hands named John put in, glancing past Dan up toward the house. "Having a pretty girlie around the place all the time will be real exciting."

Dan squared off on the man who was known to be on the lazy side and sometimes drank too much when he was in town. He was actually surprised Jack hadn't fired him during the time he'd been away, and he knew he wouldn't last much longer unless he changed his attitude. The boss wasn't going to like that at all. "Don't go getting any ideas, John."

"What? You claiming her for yourself already?" he taunted the foreman.

"No, she's Jack's daughter. That says it all. Don't even think about going near her or talking bad about her. She's a lady."

The other hands knew how serious Dan was when he used that tone of voice, and they quickly spoke up to try to ease the tension between the two men.

"It'll be good for Jack, having her here," Lou put in.

"That's right. It will be," Vic added.

"All right, get on back to work," Dan ordered.

"You are one hard-driving man, Dan Roland," Vic countered.

"That's why I've got this job," he said with a grin. He tried to make his tone easygoing, but he knew he'd have to keep an eye on John now that Penny was there. After what had happened with the man on the stage, he wasn't going to let anyone near her who had less than honorable intentions. The intensity of his need to protect her surprised him. He tried to tell himself he was only doing it for Jack, but deep within his heart he knew it was more than that. What he was feeling was more than protectiveness, more than jealousy. It was a soul-deep feeling of "right."

"If you don't mind, I think I'll go up to my room and rest for a while," Dwylah said shortly after Dan left the parlor. "I'm feeling quite exhausted."

"Of course. My cook will be up here to the house in a little while to prepare dinner. I usually eat around five or five thirty."

"Wonderful. You two enjoy your visit and I'll see you for the evening meal."

Finally alone together, Jack looked at his daughter. Things had been pleasant enough so far with the older woman in attendance, but now that they were by themselves, he had to know the truth behind all that had happened. He had to know why she hadn't responded to his letters over the years. "I've missed you," he started.

"I missed you, too. How are you? What has your doctor said about your health?" She was earnest in her need to know.

Jack was touched by her concern, but he couldn't help wondering at it after all this time. "The doc says there's nothing more he can do," he answered honestly. "It's just a matter of time now."

Penny reached out and touched his hand. "I'm sorry, Papa. I'm so sorry . . ."

"For what?" he challenged, a bit of a hard edge coming to his voice.

Penny had known there was no avoiding this moment, and she was as ready as she could ever be to explain what had happened. "I'm sorry that I never responded to your letters. I didn't know—I didn't even find out that you had been writing to me until Dan showed up."

"What do you mean?" he asked, suddenly wondering what had been going on.

"It was Mother—"

"What about her?"

"The night Dan got there and was telling me that you needed me to come home, I was confused. I hadn't heard from you in so long, and you never answered my letters, so I thought you didn't care about me anymore." She saw how his expression darkened at her words. "I didn't find out until that very night that Mother had destroyed almost all of your letters to me, and, though she told me she was mailing them, she had thrown away most of my letters to you. Aunt Matilda even admitted that she continued to do the same thing after Mother had died."

"So you never got any of my letters?" He was shocked by the harsh cruelty of what his wife had done. She had wanted to hurt him and she'd found the most painful way—she'd taken his daughter from him.

"Very few. Did you get any of mine?"

"Not many," he answered tersely, realizing even more now just how vindictive and cruel his wife had been. "I'm sorry this happened, Penny. I've been missing you all this time, but I thought you wanted nothing to do with me anymore, just like your mother."

"Oh, Papa—" She threw her arms around him and hugged him again.

Bitterness filled Jack on learning of his wife's

deceit, but at least Penny was there now, and he still had time to make up for all the lost years. He put his arms around her and held her to him. "We've missed so much, being kept apart this way. It's a good thing I sent Dan to bring you back. Why, if I'd only sent another letter—"

"Don't even think about that now. I'm here."

"Yes, you are, and there's so much I have to tell you—so much you have to learn if you're going to take over running things around here."

"You want me to take over the ranch?" She was shocked.

"Penny—"

She looked up at him in confusion and saw his deadly serious expression.

"When I die, the Lazy Ace will be yours."

"Mine . . ." Thinking of him dying brought tears to her eyes.

"Yes."

"Maybe your doctor is wrong. Maybe, you'll get better again."

"Penny." He spoke more sternly, wanting her to fully understand that he'd accepted what fate had dealt him. "I know the doc's right. I also know I don't have a lot of time left, and there's a lot I have to tell you."

"Why don't you just sell the ranch and come back to St. Louis with me? Maybe there's a doctor in the city who could help you there."

"I've worked too long and too hard to build this ranch into what it is today. The Lazy Ace is not for sale, so don't you even think about selling. You're going to take over running this ranch, and you're going to do me proud."

The fierce power of the flare of his emotions suddenly drained away, and what little strength he'd had was gone. Jack knew he had to get upstairs and lie down.

"We'll talk more later."

"Papa, are you all right?" Penny was confused.

"No, darling." He paused and looked straight at her. "I'm dying."

His words struck her like a physical blow, and she blanched under his regard.

Wearily, he got up and stood looking down at her for a moment. The look in his eyes said it all as he turned and left the room.

She got up and almost went after him, but remembering the look he'd just given her, she stayed where she was. Despite the illness that was draining his life from him, deep within him, her father was still the same commanding, proud man he'd been all those years ago.

Penny went to stare out the window, thinking of how quickly her whole life had changed all those years ago. In her mind's eye, she remembered her mother's surprising insistence that they leave on that certain day and how she'd cried when her mother had forced her into the stagecoach in town as they'd started the trip back to St. Louis. Her mother had told her she would let her come back to visit, but it had never happened.

Everything her mother had said to her had been lies—all lies.

Penny searched deep within her heart for the spirit of the young girl who'd so loved the ranch and life there, but right then she felt only emptiness and confusion inside her.

She needed someone to talk to.

Someone who would listen.

Penny left the parlor and went upstairs to softly knock on her chaperone's door.

Chapter Fifteen

Dwylah looked at Penny with open sympathy as they sat in Dwylah's bedroom talking. Having just heard what her father had told her, she could well imagine how distraught the girl was. "You have to decide what you want to do."

"I don't know anymore." Penny lifted her troubled gaze to her friend. "I thought I would come here for a visit to see my father and then probably go back to the city. I never thought Papa would want me to stay and take over the ranch. This is all so confusing. I don't know that I could go back to live with my aunt after what she did with the letters."

"Your aunt Matilda was only carrying out your mother's wishes," Dwylah told her.

"But she had to know it was wrong. Why else would she have had so much trouble being honest with me when Dan confronted her?"

"Penny, I know that hurt you deeply, but truly, it doesn't matter anymore. What matters is figuring out who you are and what you want."

"That's the trouble—everything's so complicated. I don't know who I am."

"There's no rush. You've got time. Stay here with your father and help him. That's the most important thing for right now. You can make your decision about running the ranch when the time comes."

"It will be good to get to know the ranch again," Penny said.

"Make the most of this time with your father. Get to know him again, and get to know yourself again, too. I think you may be surprised by what you discover."

Dwylah's words of wisdom touched Penny deeply. "Will you stay here with me for a while?"

"I'll be here as long as you need me."

Impulsively, Penny hugged her, appreciating her insight and wisdom. "Thank you."

Penny was feeling better as she left Dwylah and returned to her own room.

When she opened the bedroom door and discovered her room was much the way she'd left it all those years ago, she gasped in surprise. The pictures she remembered were still on the walls, the furniture was the same—the four-poster bed, dresser, and large wardrobe, and even the rug was the same. Entranced, Penny went over and spread the curtains to look out. There before her was the magnificent view of the endless miles of the Lazy Ace land that she had always loved, and she stood there for a long moment enthralled by the scene and the memories it evoked.

As she went to put her dresses in the wardrobe, she saw the shirts, riding skirts, and pants that she'd worn as a child still stored there. Her mother had refused to let her take them with her when they'd left, and her father must have kept them ever since, believing that she really was going to return someday.

Penny threw the dresses on the bed and quickly took out one of the shirts and a riding skirt. She realized that over the next few days, she was going to have to go back into town and see about getting some clothes more appropriate for ranch life. Her gowns were lovely but hardly practical.

Penny rearranged things in the wardrobe and then finished unpacking. She was going to be there for a while, so she wanted to get organized and settled in. When that was done, she lay down on her bed just to relax for a little while. The mattress and linens were new, but lying in the same four-poster bed she'd slept in growing up left her smiling up at the ceiling. In spite of all the changes in her life, some things were still the same. She closed her eyes and savored the moment.

Penny and Dwylah joined Jack for dinner in the small dining room, and Penny was glad to see that her father seemed to have gotten a bit of his strength back. They all enjoyed the meal and the conversation. Exhausted from all the hard traveling, Dwylah retired a short time later.

When the chaperone had gone upstairs, Jack looked over at his daughter.

"We need to have a talk," Jack dictated as he

pushed his chair back from the table. "Let's go in the study."

His mood had been cordial during the meal, but Penny could tell he had far more serious things on his mind now. She followed him into the room and sat down in the chair in front of his desk while he sat down at the desk.

"There are a few things you need to know," Jack began as he took out a hidden key and opened a locked desk drawer. He carefully took out some papers and placed them on the desktop. "This is my will, and everything I have I'm leaving to you."

Penny didn't say a word. She waited, knowing just by his expression that he wasn't done explaining things to her.

"There is one problem."

"What do you need, Papa? How can I help?" She was earnest in her offer.

Jack fixed his gaze on her as he began to explain, "I had meant to take care of this myself, but my health failed so quickly there was no time. I'm going to have to leave it to you to go—"

"Go where?"

"To go get my money."

"I don't understand."

"I didn't think you would, and that's why I wanted you to be here so I could explain everything." Jack got up and walked to look out the window. After a moment, he turned back to Penny and said, "I've never trusted bankers. I've seen what can happen to people when the bank they'd put their money in fails, and I vowed a long time ago I was never going to let that happen to me. I've always wanted my money right where I knew it would be, for whenever I needed it. That's why I've always kept my money here on the ranch, safely hidden where nobody could ever find it— nobody except me." Jack looked her in the eye. "Are you ready for a hard ride?"

"I guess." She was still a bit stunned by what he was telling her.

"We have to get this taken care of quickly, since I don't know how much longer I have." He picked up a sealed envelope and handed it to her. "I've written down directions to the sites where I buried the money. It won't be easy, but I'm certain you'll be able to find them."

"I'm not sure I remember the ranch as well as I used to."

"That's all right. Dan will be going with you."

Penny was surprised. "Does he know about this?"

"Not yet."

"How soon do you think I should leave?" she asked.

"As soon as possible. It's going to take you the better part of a week."

"And you trust me alone with Dan for all that time?"

Jack met her gaze straight on. "I do. He saved my life some years back, and he brought you here from St. Louis. You'll be safe with him."

"All right, but I'll need to go to town first thing in the morning to get some more suitable clothes. The clothes you kept for me upstairs are too small."

"I know," he said a bit sadly, knowing she was a woman full grown now. "You're not my 'little girl' anymore."

His words touched her and Penny got up and went to him, giving him a warm hug. "I'll always be your 'little girl,' Papa."

Jack was deeply touched by her tender embrace. He kissed her on the forehead as they moved apart. "I love you, Penny."

"I love you, too, Papa, and I'm sorry all this happened to us."

"So am I, girl. So am I. Wait here while I go get Dan."

Penny was worried about him walking all the way out to the bunkhouse, but she didn't say anything. He was determined to do it, and she wasn't about to try to stop him.

Jack checked at the small separate house that was for the foreman, but Dan wasn't there, so he made his way over to the bunkhouse. Jack walked in to find Dan sitting at the table playing cards with a few of the other hands.

"You winning or losing?" Jack joked, looking at him.

"Losing so far, but this is only my third hand."

"Cut your losses. I need you up at the house for a time."

"I'm out." Dan quickly threw in his hand and got up to leave with the boss. "I'll see you boys later."

"Hurry back," Lou called. "I like taking your money."

"I know," Dan laughed.

Jack and Dan left the bunkhouse and started up to the main house.

"I need your help, Dan."

"What's wrong?"

"Nothing's wrong," Jack said, glancing quickly around, wanting to make sure no one was anywhere close to them. "There's something I need you to do for me."

"Sure. What is it?"

"I need you to take Penny up to the box canyon."

That news did surprise him. He had no idea why he would want them to go there, and he doubted seriously that Penny was enough of a horsewoman to make the difficult ride. "Why?"

"I'll explain everything when we get inside with Penny," he told him.

They said no more as they reached the house and went into the study, where she was waiting for them.

"Evenin', Penny," Dan said as he pulled up a chair to sit beside her. "Are you all settled in?"

"Just about," she answered.

Jack went to sit back down at his desk and then looked up at the both of them. "I've already explained this to Penny, but you need to hear it, too, Dan," he began. "I've always believed in keeping my money safe."

Dan knew that was true. Jack was a very smart businessman and rancher.

"I've put a small amount in the bank in town over the years, just so nobody would suspect anything, but most of my money I've hidden, Dan, and I want you to take Penny to find it and bring it back."

"You hid your money?" Dan had had no idea.

"That's right. Up in the canyon, and I've got the map right here, showing where I put it." He pulled out his hand-drawn map and handed it to him. "Penny's going to need the money to keep the ranch going."

Dan studied his map, trying to recognize the markings he'd made. "I can go alone. It shouldn't take too long."

"No. I want Penny to go with you," Jack dictated.

When he used that tone of voice, Dan knew better than to contradict him. Still, he wondered why. Jack trusted him, and the girl would only slow him down. "All right. How soon do you want us to ride out?"

"Tomorrow afternoon," he told him. "Right, Penny?"

"I should be ready by then," she answered.

"Do you remember how to ride astride?" Jack challenged her.

"It'll come back to me," Penny countered, not wanting him to be disappointed in her.

Dan didn't breathe a word as he waited to see what Jack would say next.

"All right. You heard her, Dan. She'll be ready to go in the afternoon."

Dan handed him back the map. "I'll be ready, too."

"I want you to hurry. The weather could change at any time—and Christmas is coming." He gave his daughter a loving look. "We're going to spend Christmas together this year."

"Yes, Papa. We are.

"I'd better get upstairs and get some rest," Penny said. She had a feeling the two men needed to talk business for a while, so she went to kiss her father on the cheek and then left them alone.

When she'd disappeared upstairs, Jack looked back at his foreman. "I know this won't be easy for you, but you're the only one I can trust with her. There's no way she can make the ride up to the canyon on her own."

"Are you sure you don't want me to go alone? I can probably get back quicker without her. You heard what she said—she hasn't really ridden much, living in the city."

Jack met his gaze straight on. His expression was serious, but Dan saw a glimmer of something else in his eyes.

"That's why she has to go. I want to be sure she can make the ride. The daughter I raised was feisty and brave. She was capable of handling just about anything—or anybody. I don't know what's happened to her these last years living away from here with her mother. But I have to make sure my Penny is still there."

"All right, Jack. We'll do it," Dan promised.

"Yes," Jack said with certainty. "You will."

To get a smile out of Jack, Dan asked, "Should I take Dwylah with us? She's our chaperone, you know."

The thought of the chaperone trying to ride one of their horses did make him smile. "What if I said yes?"

"We could take her along, but we might not get back until the spring thaw."

"There's a line shack or two up there."

They finally laughed a bit. Then Jack's mood sobered again.

"I trust you, Dan. If anybody can take care of my girl, it's you. Bring her back safe and sound—and get the money."

"I will," he told him.

Dan left him then. He, too, knew he was going to need some sleep that night, for he sure wouldn't be getting much, camping out with Penny up in the canyon this next week.

As Dan came out of the main house and headed back to the small house that served as the foreman's home, he didn't see John lurking in the shadows near the study window.

John stayed down and out of sight until Dan had gone into his place and closed the door. Only then did the ranch hand emerge from the darkness and return to the bunkhouse.

Something big was going on.

He knew it.

John had been just coming out of the stable when he'd seen Jack and Dan leave the bunkhouse. They hadn't noticed him, and he'd been glad. He hadn't been able to hear everything they were talking about, but it had sounded intriguing, so he'd sneaked over by the study window to try to listen in.

When John had heard Jack say there was some money hidden up in the canyon, he'd gotten real interested. He hated working on this ranch, and he didn't have any use for the foreman. Dan had it in for him, always giving him the hardest, dirtiest jobs to do and staying on him constantly. John knew this would be the perfect chance to get even—and get rich. He was supposed to ride out and check stock for the next few days, and that gave him the opportunity he needed to head for the canyon instead. Since they weren't leaving until the afternoon, he could ride out to the canyon area and hide out, while he waited for them to show up. He'd find the money, and then be long gone before anyone even found out he was involved.

Chapter Sixteen

Penny went to speak with Dwylah the first thing the next morning.

"You're doing what?" Dwylah asked, shocked after hearing about her father's hidden money.

"I have to ride up to the canyon with Dan."

"Will you be back tonight?"

"No. We'll probably be gone at least a few days."

"Oh my goodness—" The chaperone wasn't sure what to do.

"What I wanted to tell you was, right after breakfast I'm going into town to get some work clothes and I wondered if you wanted to go with me? The dresses I've got aren't quite suitable for any hard riding," she explained.

"I've never been one to pass up a shopping trip," Dwylah answered, smiling back. "But tell me, could this trip to the canyon be dangerous?"

"Dan will be with me. I'll be safe," she assured her.

"Danny will keep you safe, but I'd better get riding clothes, too, so I can go with you. I am the chaperone, you know."

Penny couldn't help herself. The thought of

Dwylah riding astride up to the canyon was humorous enough, but she knew what her true motive was. Penny started to laugh. "I know why you really want to go—you just want to spend more time with Dan."

Dwylah laughed, too. "I'd never pass up the chance."

Penny knew she had to discourage her from going. "It's a hard ride, though. I'm a little concerned about making the ride myself. It's been so long since I've ridden astride, but we're in a hurry and we have to get up there and get back."

"But you're going to be alone with Danny," Dwylah pointed out.

"This is important. I have to do it. I'm not worried about my reputation. We're not in society anymore. We're back on the ranch, and I'm taking care of my father's business."

"There's nothing else you can do, is there?"

"No. My father's not strong enough to make the trip. I have to go."

"Well, let's get into town while you have time."

They found Jack waiting for them downstairs.

"Breakfast is ready. You won't want to go into town without eating something," he told them.

They all went into the kitchen to eat.

"We'll be back as soon as possible, Papa," Penny assured him.

"Get whatever you need and tell Artie to put it on my bill," Jack advised. "Take an extra blanket with you this morning. Rob's taking you in the buckboard. He's picking up supplies while you're there."

Penny went upstairs to get another blanket and their coats. When she came back down, she saw that Rob had pulled up out in front.

"Rob's ready to leave," Jack told them.

They went outside to find the older ranch hand waiting for them with the buckboard.

"So we're going in that?" Dwylah eyed the buckboard skeptically. It looked to be a much rougher ride than the carriage that had brought them out to the ranch.

"Do you want to stay here?" Penny asked, knowing it wouldn't be an easy ride for her.

"No, I'm always ready for something new. Let's go!" Dwylah went down to where Rob was standing.

Rob helped Dwylah up on to the driver's bench first, knowing she'd be safest sitting in the middle between him and Penny. After getting Penny seated, he joined them there.

"We'll be back soon, Papa," Penny promised as they started off.

Jack stood on the porch, watching them drive away. Dan had been down at the stable, and when he saw Jack, he came over to talk with him. They had a lot of plans to make, and this was the time. He had to get their supplies and be ready to leave when Penny returned from town. They went inside to talk.

"Are you ready for this?" Jack asked Dan as they settled in his office.

"We'll do it," he assured him.

"Just keep an eye on her. Penny could be trouble. She always was as a child," Jack told him with a half smile, remembering some of the wilder escapades of her younger years.

"I thought I'd put her on Ol' Midnight."

"That's good. He'll be an easy, steady ride for her."

"I'm going to go get things packed up. Let me know when she's ready to head out."

"I will, and, Dan—" Jack's tone turned serious as his foreman looked his way. "Be careful."

"Yes, sir."

Dan left him then, his thoughts a bit troubled. He was making this trip for Jack, just like he'd made the trip back to St. Louis, but this time he was going to be alone with Penny out in the middle of nowhere. He hoped she was capable of keeping up with him, but lady that she was, he had his doubts. It wasn't going to be easy, no matter what he'd told Jack. She was a temptation, and he was going to have to concentrate on the job he'd been sent to do, and nothing else.

"Oh my—" Was all Dwylah could say as she stared at Penny.

Penny had gone in a back room of the general store to try on the work clothes she needed for out at the ranch. She stood before her now, wearing a pair of denim pants, boots, a boy's work shirt, and a cowboy hat.

"What do you think?" Penny asked.

"I never thought I'd see you wearing pants," she answered, realizing how they showed off the slender curves of her figure. She might be wearing clothes fit for a boy, but she certainly didn't look like one.

"I picked out a riding skirt, too, but the pants will be warmer."

"I see," she replied, but she was having trouble adjusting to this part of western life. "You will need a heavier coat, won't you? The one you wore on the trip back from St. Louis certainly won't work if you're out riding."

"You're right."

"I've got what you need right here, Penny," Mrs. Carson, the shopkeeper's wife said, coming to speak with them, carrying a suitable work coat. "It's a boy's size, but it looks like it'll fit you." She'd known Penny before she'd left, and was impressed with the woman she'd become. She was surprised she wanted to get back to the ranch life after living in the city for so long, but Penny was, after all, Jack Anderson's daughter, and that explained it.

Penny quickly put the coat on and was satisfied it would work. "I'll need another pair of pants and another shirt."

"I'll get them for you right away."

Penny went in back and, to Dwylah's surprise, came out still dressed in work clothes, carrying the clothes she'd worn to town.

"You aren't going to change back for the trip home?" she asked.

"There's no need," she answered. "Dan and I will be leaving right after we get there, so I might as well just stay like this."

Rob had already loaded up the supplies he was taking back, and had been watching for them. He met them at the buckboard. He stared at Jack's daughter as if seeing a complete stranger. She definitely didn't look like a fancy city girl anymore, dressed as she was. She looked like she was ready to hire on at the Lazy Ace.

"Do you need anything else here in town, Penny?" Rob asked.

"No. Papa's waiting. We have to get back."

He helped Dwylah up and was about to help Penny when she climbed up agilely all by herself to the driver's bench. He took his seat and grabbed up the reins, set for the trip back.

The ride back to the ranch was cold, but uneventful. Jack had been watching for them and he came out of the study just as Penny and Dwylah entered the house. He stopped to stare at his daughter and ended up smiling.

"Don't you look like a ranch hand," he said.

"That's what I was aiming for," she replied. "I've got a job to do, and I'm going to do it."

"Yes, you are."

Rob had followed them inside, carrying their bags for them,

"Go find Dan for me," Jack told him.

"I'll send him right up," Rob said. He left the house to look for the foreman and found him working with Vic in the stable.

"Jack said to tell you he needs you up at the house."

"Thanks, Rob."

When Dan had gone, Rob saw the horses that were saddled and waiting, and he looked to Vic. "Is Dan riding out?"

Vic repeated what Dan had told him. "He's taking Penny out to show her around the ranch. Jack wants her to get a feel for things while the weather's holding up."

"Dan is one lucky man," Rob said.

"Why do you say that?" Vic didn't envy Dan the task of riding around the Lazy Ace with a city girl.

"You should see that girlie now. She's all dressed up like a real cowgirl, all ready for trouble. Or maybe she is trouble," he chuckled. His tone didn't leave any doubt about what kind of "trouble" he meant.

Rob didn't know that Lou had walked up behind him as he was talking to Vic.

Lou's expression was threatening as he faced down the ranch hand. "You're talking about the boss's daughter, Rob. Remember that."

Rob shut up and went to take care of the team and the buckboard, but he was still thinking Dan was going to have a fine time with Penny.

Dan knocked on the front door and heard Jack call for him to come in.

"I'm in the study."

Dan went down the hall and came to a stop in the study doorway. Dan always prided himself on his ability to control his reactions, and he was real proud of the way he kept his expression blank when he got his first look at Penny wearing her ranching clothes. He'd thought she was gorgeous in her gowns, but seeing her dressed liked this, he thought she was even prettier.

"Do you think these clothes will work for the ride?" Penny asked in her innocence.

"They'll do much better than your dresses," Dan assured her. "Are you ready to leave?"

"We were going to have some lunch first. You want to join us? There's no sense in you riding out hungry," Jack invited.

"I appreciate the offer, Jack, but I've still got a few things to take care of down at the stable. How soon will you be done eating?"

"About half an hour," Jack said.

"Just let me know, and we'll be ready to ride out." Dan left them to finish taking care of business.

Jack went with Penny to join Dwylah, who was already waiting for them at the table.

The meal was hot and tasty, and Penny had a good idea this would be her last decent meal for quite a few days.

"Is there anything else I need to know before we leave?"

"Just listen to Dan," Jack advised. "He's a good man and he knows what he's doing."

"I will," she promised. She paused for a moment, and then asked, "Papa, there is one thing I wanted to ask you about."

"What?"

"Do I need to take a gun along?" She remembered the shooting lessons he'd given her years before, and though she hadn't fired a gun since she'd left the ranch, she knew trouble could show up anywhere, at any time on the Lazy Ace.

Jack was thoughtful for a moment and then got up and left the room. He returned with a gun belt and sidearm. "There's no need for you to be wearing it, but you can put it in your saddlebags. That way you'll have it just in case you do run into trouble." He put it on the table next to her.

Dwylah stared at the gun for a moment and then looked at Penny. "You actually know how to use that?"

"It's been a while, but yes, Papa taught me when I was young."

"Oh my—"

Jack looked to Dwylah. "I always wanted my girl to be able to take care of herself."

"I can see that."

"This isn't the city," he added.

"Obviously."

They finished eating, and Penny hurried upstairs to pack what she needed to take along. She tied her hair back, put on her new coat and hat. She took a quick glance in the mirror and was satisfied that her father would be proud of her.

She definitely looked like she belonged on the Lazy Ace now.

She was back.

Grabbing up the bag she was taking along, she left her room and started down the hall. She reached the top of the stairs to find Dan, Dwylah, and her father talking in the hall below.

Jack went to meet her at the bottom of the steps and gave her a quick hug. "I gave Dan the map, and your gun is in your saddlebag."

"Thank you, Papa."

"Listen to me, Penny. Do whatever Dan tells you to do. He knows his way around the Lazy Ace. Trust him—and be careful," Jack dictated. "You never know what kind of trouble you might run into out there."

"We'll be careful," she assured him, and then she gave him another hug before turning to Dwylah to give her one, too. "I know Papa is worried about me getting in trouble, but I want to know if you're going to keep an eye on him while we're gone. He might prove to be more trouble for you than I was on the trip."

"I'll try, but I don't think it will be easy," Dwylah

said, smiling brightly at her and Jack. "He is, after all, your father."

"Don't you worry about me, Penny," Jack
laughed. "I'll be right here waiting for you when
you get back."

"I'm counting on that, Papa. We'll hurry. Christmas is less than two weeks away. I want to spend
it with you." She kissed his cheek.

At the stables, Dan brought out a deep black
horse.

"You'll be riding Ol' Midnight," Dan said as he
untied the reins and handed them to Penny. He
stepped back to watch her mount and was impressed when she swung easily up into the saddle.
He found it hard to believe this was the same girl
he'd tracked down in the city at the dance. "You
all right?"

Penny nodded as she got comfortable

Dan mounted his own horse and took up his
reins. Looking to Jack, he told him, "We'll be back
as soon as possible."

"I'm counting on it," Jack said.

Chapter Seventeen

Dan glanced over to see how Penny was handling the horse. He knew right away she hadn't forgotten how to ride, and that was real good news, considering the long miles they had ahead of them. "Are you comfortable on Ol' Midnight?"

"He's fine."

"Good."

"How far is it to the canyon?"

"We should make it by tomorrow afternoon. There's a line shack about halfway up, so we'll spend the night there tonight."

"That's going to be a lot better than camping out," she said, trying to imagine sleeping around a campfire in the cold.

"We've been lucky so far with the weather, but that could change real fast. If a blue norther comes through, we'll be needing a whole lot more blankets than what we brought along."

"I remember how bad they can be," she agreed. "One time I think the temperature dropped more than fifty degrees in less than an hour and then it started snowing, too."

"Blue northers are rough, that's for sure. Let's just hope the weather stays decent long enough so we can find everything your father sent us after."

"I get the feeling this isn't going to be easy."

"Your pa never does anything the easy way, but that's why the Lazy Ace is so successful. In the years I've worked for him, I've never seen him back down from any challenge."

"You're right. I don't think he's ever been afraid of anything."

"There was one thing—" Dan started

She glanced over at him, surprised and curious. "Really? What was it?"

"He was afraid you wouldn't come back to the ranch. That's why he sent me to get you rather than just writing another letter or sending a wire. He knew I wouldn't come back without you."

"So you're never afraid of a challenge, either?" she asked, casting him a quick sidelong smile.

He shook his head and smiled wryly. "Not anymore. I've learned that challenges just mean you have to work harder, that's all."

Even as he said it, though, Dan knew he was facing one of his biggest challenges ever, being out alone with her this way for almost a week. He told himself he was riding with her to help her and to protect her, and he knew he would, but she was proving to be a temptation he was finding harder and harder to resist. He'd overcome serious challenges in the past, and he was confident he could do it again.

"My father got himself a good foreman when he hired you."

"I like to think so. I do my best for him. He's a fine man."

All the lies and negative things her mother had said about her father over the years had haunted her during their time apart, and Penny knew she was going to have to put all of that behind her and try to be the loving daughter she once was. Eager to prove herself ready to take up where she had left off, she urged her horse to an even faster pace.

Dan was surprised by her action and spurred his horse on, catching up with her quickly. "Where do you think you're going?"

"Up to the canyon," she said with confidence. "We're going to find that money and get back to the ranch. I want to spend all the time with my father as I can."

"I understand what you mean." And he did. It seemed to Dan everything he'd believed about her in the beginning was being proven wrong. She wasn't the spoiled little girl he'd expected her to be when he'd first seen her at the ball. It would have been real easy for her to have stayed in St. Louis and sent him on back to the ranch alone, but when she'd learned about the deception that had kept her away from her father all this time, she'd proven that she still loved him and wanted to put things right between them. Dan admired her for that. The irritation he'd felt with her early on for going back East and leaving the father who loved her was over. She realized what she'd lost and she wanted it back.

He knew she was one lucky girl.

Not everyone had the chance to reclaim what they'd lost.

It was getting close to dinnertime when Jack came to join Dwylah in the parlor.

"I wonder how Penny's holding up, riding astride the way she is," Dwylah said. "That can't be easy for her after all these years of living in the city."

"The first day or two will be hard for her, but she'll get used to it. She's my girl," he said.

"Yes, she is. I'm amazed at how quickly she seemed to adapt to everything here again. Back in St. Louis she would never have been caught wearing pants and riding astride." She was glad he was proud of his daughter.

"Did you know Elizabeth very well?" Jack asked.

"I did socialize with your wife, but I'm actually closer friends with her sister, Matilda. That's why I volunteered to come along with Penny. They were desperate, and Matilda knew she could trust me."

"That was very kind of you to make the trip, and you did a find job, by the way. Penny showed up safe and sound."

"Danny had a lot to do with that, too. He's a good man, your Danny."

"I wish he were 'my Danny.' I'd be proud to claim him as my son. He's been a big help here on the Lazy Ace. But what about you—do you do this sort of thing very often? It can't be an easy job being the chaperone and traveling across the country this way."

"Actually, I've never done anything like this before. I was excited by the thought of coming to Texas. I've always heard about what it was like to live on a ranch, but I wanted to see if for real. It seems like it's quite an adventure."

"You haven't been here very long yet, but what do you think of the Lazy Ace so far?"

"I love it. You've done a wonderful job here. You must be proud of the way things have turned out."

"I am, and I hope Penny feels the same way. I want her to take over the ranch and run it, once I'm gone."

Dwylah had had a feeling that might be his plan. "Do you think that's a wise decision?"

Jack was surprised by her reaction. "Of course."

"I know Penny's an intelligent young woman, but for her to take over running a big ranch like this one . . . Well, I don't know if she's ready for that much responsibility. She's never done anything like this before."

"If things go the way I hope they will, everything will turn out just fine."

Dwylah thought he sounded very confident and when she saw the look in his eyes, she couldn't help wondering at it. "What do you mean? Is there something you aren't telling us?"

"No," he answered honestly. "But I think it's real good that Penny and Dan are making this ride up to the canyon together. That's all."

She suddenly realized what his motive had been for sending them up to the canyon the way he had, and she nodded in understanding. The way she felt about Danny, she found herself smiling at his plan. "It's no wonder you're so successful, Jack. You do know how to make things happen."

"I try." He grinned at her.

"Danny is a fine man. Penny could do far worse."

"I take it they got along on the trip here?"

"Yes, they did. I've been impressed with him ever since he came for her at the Chase ball. If Danny wants something, nothing stops him from doing what he has to do to get it. He's one very intelligent, resourceful young man."

"That's right. Dan has proven himself to be smart and loyal, and I've found those to be the two finest qualities in a man—especially in a man I'd like to see as my son-in-law."

"You're a conniver, Jack Anderson!" Dwylah was giggling.

"Yes, I am," he answered, not even bothering to try to argue with her.

"Well, I hope your plan works out," she said. She smiled to herself then, thinking how wonderful it would be if they did fall in love and get married. Of course, she wanted to be the one who got Danny to the justice of the peace, but if she couldn't have him, she wanted Penny to be the one.

"Do you play chess?" Jack asked, finding her company quite entertaining.

"I've managed to win a game or two in my time," she answered, not revealing how good she really was.

"Let's play a game. I have the board in my office."

"I'd love to."

She followed him from the parlor and took one last look out the window at the endless miles of the ranch land, and wondered just where Penny and Danny were right then.

It was getting close to dark when Dan and Penny finally reined in at the line shack.

"We're halfway to the canyon," he announced as he dismounted and tied up his horse to the hitching rail.

Penny managed to keep herself from moaning as she got down off Ol' Midnight. The horse had been a good choice for her. He had kept up with Dan and his pace had been steady, but even so, she was definitely realizing her muscles weren't quite used to the ranching life yet.

Dan glanced her way and saw the slightly pained look on her face, and he couldn't help grinning. "Little bit of a hard ride for you today?"

"I thought the buckboard was rough, but that was nothing compared to hours in the saddle. I've got to toughen up if I'm going to last out here."

"You will. I have confidence in you."

"I know, I know—I'm my father's daughter," she came back at him, managing a pained laugh.

Penny went into the shack and took a look around. Starkly furnished, it was equipped with just the basics that the ranch hands would need when they were out working stock. There were two sets of bunk beds, a small table with four chairs crammed in between the beds leaving just enough room to walk around, and a small stove for cooking and heating.

Dan followed her in carrying some wood for the stove. "Let me get a fire started and then I'll take care of the horses."

"Do you need any help with them?"

"No, but you can make the beds when I bring our gear."

"I think I can handle that job."

"Good. Maybe the boss will hire you on," he joked. "We can always use another good hand on the ranch."

"I'll have to have a talk with him when we get back."

"You do that," he agreed as he put the wood in the stove and started the fire. Once he was sure it was safely lit, he went outside and brought in his rifle, their bedrolls and saddlebags, and her extra bag. He put all their gear on the table.

Penny was ready to make his bed first. Dan was just starting back outside to take care of the horses when she called out to him, "Dan, do you like being on top or the bottom?"

Dan was concentrating on trying to get everything done before dark, and her question took him by surprise. He stopped and looked back at her, his gaze raking over her as she stood there in all her innocence holding his bedroll. He knew she had no idea of the images her question had aroused in him, and he also knew he had to put those thoughts right out of his mind.

"On top," he answered, and he hurried on to take care of the horses. Being back out in the cold would help right then.

Penny made their bunks and then took out enough food for their meal. When she saw the food they had for their dinner, she was glad she'd eaten lunch earlier that day. Ranch hands were hardworking men, and now she understood why they were always glad to get back to the main house and eat the hot meals the cook was serving up. She was going to feel the same way when they got back from the canyon. She lit the lamp that was on the table and waited for Dan to return.

Dan tended to the horses and came back up to the shack with a bucket of water for washing up and for making coffee.

"It's getting colder out there. The wind is picking up," he said as he shut the door tightly behind him. He stopped to take off his coat. The welcoming warmth of the room and the sight of her standing there in the soft glow of the lamp light left him with a feeling like he had come home, and the reaction surprised him. He'd been on his own for so long that he hadn't thought much about having a home and a family—until now.

Penny found herself mesmerized as she watched him shrug out of his coat. The broad width of his shoulders left no doubt about how strong he was, and there was an aura of masculinity about him that left her acutely conscious of his nearness there in the close confines of the line shack.

"How far do we have to ride tomorrow?" Penny asked as they sat down to eat their dinner.

Dan took the map out of his shirt pocket and spread it on the table for her to see. The drawing Jack had made was simple enough, but Dan knew someone not familiar with the canyon wouldn't have any idea where to start looking.

Penny studied it for a long moment and then looked up at Dan across the table. "I'm glad you're riding with me. I recognize a few things Papa's drawn there, but I wouldn't have any chance at all of finding the money on my own."

"I'm sure he planned it that way. We should be able to make it to the first site sometime tomorrow afternoon. Then it will be about another half day's ride to the second place."

"It feels like we're hunting for a buried treasure."

Dan looked up at her. "We are. Knowing Jack, I'm sure this is no small amount of money, and you're going to need all of it to keep the Lazy Ace going." He noticed how her expression got more serious at his words. "What's troubling you?"

Penny wasn't sure she should say anything yet, but knowing her father trusted him she told him, "I don't know if I can keep the Lazy Ace going after Papa . . ." She paused for a moment, emotion choking her. "After Papa is gone. I've been away for so long, and I know so little about actually running a ranch as big as this one. The ranch hands aren't going to listen to me. I probably should sell it and go back to St. Louis. That would be best for everybody."

Dan couldn't believe what he was hearing. He knew if she did that after Jack died, Jack would be turning over in his grave. "Your father would never have considered putting you in charge of the Lazy Ace unless he believed you were capable of taking over and running things. He trusts that you can do it. You should trust yourself."

Penny shrugged and looked away, her thoughts in turmoil.

"Penny—I believe you can do it."

"You do?" She glanced at him, shocked.

"That's right. I admit I had my doubts back in St. Louis. I didn't know how the girl I found at the dance was going to react to the idea of leaving the good life she had in the city to take up living on a ranch again. I was worried—for your father's sake—but I've been watching you and I've been impressed. You are Jack's daughter, and you're doing him proud."

"You really think so?"

"Yes, I do, and, Penny . . ." He waited until she met his gaze. He saw the doubt, confusion, and uncertainty in her eyes. "This is your home. Don't ever forget that."

Something stirred deep within her at his words, and she felt a sense of pride strengthen her. "You're right, Dan. I am my father's daughter. I've got work to do here on the Lazy Ace."

"Yes, you do, so you'd better get some rest tonight. Tomorrow is going to be an even harder day in the saddle for you." He knew how sore she was going to be in the morning.

"You're right about that," she agreed, getting up slowly from her chair to clean off the table. "I can only imagine what I'd be feeling like right now if I'd been on a different horse."

While she washed the dishes, Dan checked the stove and added more wood to it to keep things warm overnight.

"Do you need some time alone to get ready for bed?" he asked, wanting to give her the privacy she needed.

Penny looked up, a little unsettled by the thought

of the night to come. "Just a few minutes, if you don't mind."

"All right. I'll go check on the horses and be right back."

Penny took care of her needs and then thought about changing into the heavy flannel nightgown she'd brought along. As cold as the night was turning out to be, though, she realized she'd be better off just sleeping in her clothes. She took off her boots and climbed into the bottom bunk, opposite the bunks where Dan would be sleeping.

When he came back in a short time later, he found her curled up in her blankets on her bed.

"You need anything else?" he asked.

"No, thank you."

"I guess I'll get up on top, then," he said, smiling to himself.

Penny watched as Dan sat down on the other bottom bunk and took off his boots. Then he turned out the lamp and climbed up into the top bunk to settle down. She waited a minute, listening to the harsh gusts of the wind outside, before she told him, "Thanks, Dan."

"For what?"

"For helping my father—and me. There's no way I could have made this trip on my own in this kind of weather."

"You're welcome. Now get some sleep."

"You, too," she returned. She thought he

sounded grouchy and, though it puzzled her, she just figured it was probably because he was tired. She rolled over and, huddling beneath her blankets, she sought warmth and rest.

Dan was still cold as he lay in his solitary bunk. Earlier, being "on top" had sounded good, but now he knew it wasn't. He glanced down to where she was nestled on the other bottom bunk, and he found himself wishing he could climb down there and take her in his arms. He knew they would both be a whole lot warmer if he did.

Dan still found it hard to believe that Jack trusted him enough to let him make this trip alone with Penny. He tried to imagine Dwylah making the ride with them, and he knew they wouldn't have gotten very far with the chaperone along. Even so, it was a great responsibility, being here in the line shack with Penny. He thought about their conversation about being on top again and grimaced, shifting positions so he was facing the wall away from her.

Dan closed his eyes.

Morning was going to be there real fast.

He just hoped he could get some sleep.

Chapter Eighteen

"If the weather holds, we'll be in Sagebrush in a few more days," the stage driver said as they sat at the table in the way station having a late dinner. They'd had some damage to one of the wheels and had fallen behind schedule. "Sorry we're running late, but some things can't be helped."

"We're just blessed no one was injured," Nick said, knowing how serious things could have been had the stage been wrecked.

"You're right about that, Reverend," he agreed. "I'm thinking it pays to have a preacher man riding with me this trip."

"So, are all you folks going to be home in time for Christmas?" Andy, the manager of the station, asked as he came back inside after taking care of things down at the stable.

The little boy named Zach spoke up, smiling brightly. "We are! It won't be long now, will it, Mama?"

"No, it won't. We're going to have a wonderful Christmas this year," his mother said.

"Santa is coming! I know he's going to bring me presents this year 'cause I've been good, haven't I?"

"Yes, Zach, you've been very good." His father smiled at him.

"I can't wait to get home!"

Santa Claus—

Presents—

Home—

Steve was sitting between Nick and Miss Lacey at the table, listening to the other boy. The boy and his parents had been traveling with them for the last two days, and they'd been much better company than the other man and woman who'd been so mean to Miss Lacey when she'd first got on the stage. Even so, all the talk about Santa Claus and the joy of spending Christmas with his family left Steve feeling miserable. He would never again be with his mother and father on Christmas, and he had no idea if Santa would even know where to begin to look to find him and bring him any presents this year.

Steve didn't let on about his heartache. He just stayed quiet and tried to concentrate on eating his beans and bacon. He told himself he was being an adventurer, making this long trip with Reverend Miller. The excitement that had filled him until now, though, faded away, and he was left with only the realization that he would never be able to go back to the days when he was surrounded by a loving family.

Andy started to clear the table as some of the adults finished their meals. As he took away Nick's place, he frowned, staring at him.

"Is something wrong?" Nick asked, puzzled by his expression.

"No, nothing's wrong. I just recognized you, that's all."

Nick was surprised. "We've met before?"

"Yeah, you just were through here not too long ago, weren't you?"

"No. This is the first time I've traveled this way." Hope suddenly flared within him.

"Well, you look a lot like a fella who came through here on his way to Sagebrush."

"Do you remember his name?" Nick asked, a bit excited.

"No, I get too many people through here to keep track."

"My brother, Dan Roland, was traveling this way, too, so it might have been him."

"Could have been." Andy moved off to take care of business.

Glad to be distracted from his own sadness, Steve looked up at Reverend Miller. "He was here!"

Nick smiled down at him. "I hope so, Steve. If it was Danny, we'll be catching up to him real soon."

Lacey smiled, too. "Your long trip will all have been worth it, once you find him."

"Yes, it will," Nick agreed. Over the days of traveling together, he'd found Lacey to be a very smart young woman. It was obvious she was a survivor. They'd had no chance to talk privately, but he'd been impressed with how she'd conducted herself around the young boys. He believed there was a lady inside her, and he hoped he could help her find a way to improve her life.

It was a short time later the women started to retire to their separate room.

"Wait!" Zach ran to his mother to give her a good night hug. "Good night, Mama."

"Good night and sleep tight," she said, lovingly kissing his cheek.

Steve pretended not to notice. He went with Reverend Miller to get ready for bed. As harsh as the accommodations were, they all knew they were fortunate that the stage had been able to make it to the way station. It would have been a cold, hard night, if they'd been forced to sleep on the stage.

Steve took the cot beside the reverend and curled up on his side, facing away from him. He didn't want Reverend Miller to know how listening to the other boy was affecting him.

And yet alone in the darkness, Steve was filled with sorrow and he couldn't stop himself from crying. He wept as quietly as he could, but feared one of the men would wake up and hear him. Taking great care, Steve got up from his cot and crept from the room. He made his way to the front door and grabbed his coat and went outside.

The night was cold, but Steve just wanted to be alone with his misery. He made his way to the side of the station and hunkered down against the building. He cried his heart out, knowing he had no one to spend Christmas with and knowing no one loved him the way his parents had loved him.

Inside the station, Lacey had been trying to get to sleep. The other woman had drifted off right away, but Lacey found herself staring at the ceiling, worrying about the fact that they were almost to Sagebrush. The driver had said just a few more days. Soon she would be left all alone in a strange town with little money and no friends. She'd been in bad situations before and she'd survived. All she had to do was find a job to support herself and things would be all right.

Even as Lacey thought it, though, she knew she was limited on the type of work she could get. She wasn't much of a cook, but she figured she could probably wait on tables if there was a restaurant there in town. She certainly didn't want to risk going to work in a saloon again. She would work hard for her money, but the work had to be respectable. She would work as a laundress or a maid if she had to.

Firmly resolved, Lacey felt a little more at peace and had just rolled over to try to fall asleep when she heard it—the distant, muffled sound of someone crying.

Lacey got out of bed and moved over to the window, and it was there she could hear the weeping more clearly. Though she couldn't see anyone outside, she had a real good feeling it was Steve. She'd noticed how he'd gotten quiet when the other boy had been talking about Santa Claus and being back home for Christmas, so she knew he needed some support right then. Lacey had slept in her clothes, so all she had to do was slip on her coat and boots and sneak out of the room to go check on the orphan.

The main room was deserted and the lamps had been put out, but there was enough light coming from the fireplace so she could see. She tiptoed across the room and as silently as she could, she opened the door and crept out into the cold, dark night. She quickly closed the door behind her and made her way to the side of the house.

She came around the corner to find Steve. She thought about going to get Reverend Miller, and then changed her mind. She decided to follow her instincts instead. She knew right then the boy needed love, and she did love him. He was sweet and adorable and resourceful, and she wanted him to know that she truly did care about him. Without saying a word, Lacey went to him.

When someone knelt beside him and put an arm around him, Steve was startled, for he had not heard anyone coming.

"Steve, it's me—Miss Lacey," she said in a quiet voice as she drew him to her.

"I'm all right. I'll go back inside," he managed, choking on his words as he tried to stop crying.

"Steve, if you want to cry, go ahead," Lacey told him gently. She held him to her heart, and she felt the misery in him as he stayed rigid for a moment in her arms. "It's all right."

At her tender words, Steve collapsed against her, all pretense gone. "I miss my mama and my papa so much—and it's almost Christmas—" His breath hitched.

Lacey knew there was nothing she could say right then that would make things better. She just held him close and let him weep. He just clung to her, drawing on the solace she was offering.

When the cold started to get to her, she brushed his tousled hair and kissed his forehead. "We'd better get back inside. I don't want you getting sick."

"All right," he said hoarsely.

Lacey got up and drew him up with her. Keeping her arm around him, she guided him back inside. "Next time you get lonely, just remember there are people who love you very much. I know I do." She gave him a squeeze. "You get some rest now."

He looked up at her, his eyes red and swollen from his tears, and he nodded. Then he stood on tiptoes and pressed a quick kiss to her cheek. "I love you, too, Miss Lacey."

She had never heard a more heartrending declaration of love, and she watched him as he moved off back to the men's sleeping area. She stayed there a few minutes longer, wanting to make sure he didn't have any trouble. Only when she was sure he was safe did she return to the women's room.

Lacey knew Steve was a special child, and she was going to have a talk with the reverend about him as soon as she could find a moment alone with him. Steve needed help, and she was going to do whatever she could for him. She knew what it was like to be alone in the world, and she didn't want him suffering this way at his young age. Somehow, she had to find a way to bring peace and joy back into his life.

Lacey thought about all he'd said to her that night and knew that once they got to Sagebrush she was going to have to find him a present for Christmas. Santa Claus couldn't miss a good boy like Steve.

Chapter Nineteen

It was early morning and John was hidden out behind some big boulders halfway up the hillside behind the line shack. He kept watch as Dan and Penny came outside and mounted up, and he couldn't help smiling when he wondered what had gone on inside there overnight. Jack's daughter was a real looker, and Dan would have been a fool not to take advantage of her while he had the chance. He knew he certainly would have enjoyed himself if he'd been alone with her all night.

John waited until Dan and Penny had ridden out and then he saddled up and trailed slowly after them. He was glad Penny was riding with the foreman. Though she could handle a horse, she was slowing Dan down and that made it easier for him to stay after them. The terrain in the canyon was rugged, and that helped John, too, for he needed to stay out of sight.

John wished he could have gotten a look at the map that showed where the money was buried, but there had been no way. As it was, he was forced to bide his time and lie back and trail them. John was glad he didn't have to worry about showing up at the ranch. No one expected him back for at least three more days. Not that he'd ever be back once he got the money. He'd hightail it out and then live the life of a high roller.

John could hardly wait.

"How much farther is it?" Penny asked as she rode behind Dan on the steep, rocky, winding trail. After several hours in the saddle, they had to be getting close.

"Probably another two or three miles," he answered. "Are you doing all right?"

"Yes, though it's hard to believe that it was just a few weeks ago I was at the Chase ball. It's seems like an eternity—almost like another life."

She wondered what Richard and Amanda would think of her now if they saw her bundled up against the cold in workman's clothes, riding astride out in the middle of nowhere. She remembered how attentive Richard had been that night and now it all seemed like a fairy tale.

Fairy tale—

She let her gaze linger on Dan, seeing the day's growth of beard on his jawline and liking how it added an aura of danger about him. She hadn't even realized she'd needed saving when he'd whisked her away from the ballroom. But without him, she wouldn't have been reunited with her father. There was no denying Dan, that was for sure.

Penny urged her mount forward to ride beside him as the trail widened.

"Do you miss being in the city?" he asked.

"I miss my friends, but being back here with Papa means a lot to me."

Dan wondered if one of the friends she was missing was the man she'd been dancing with when he'd showed up at the ball. His chest felt tight at the thought of her in another man's arms. "Let's take another look at that map," he said to get his mind off how much he wanted to hold her close. "The sooner we find your father's money, the sooner we can get back."

Dwylah was never content to sit around and do nothing, and as the day wore on, she grew restless. Jack had been locked in his office, going over his books and doing paperwork, so she had been left to her own devices. She sought out Lou's wife, Josie, who did the cooking and cleaning for Jack, and found her hard at work in the kitchen.

"I wanted to ask you—" Dwylah began.

"What is it?" Josie asked, looking up from where she was washing dishes.

"Does Jack ever decorate for the holidays?"

Josie shook her head sadly as she wiped her hands on a towel. "No, not anymore. He hasn't bothered with any Christmas decorations in years."

"I think this year, we're going to have to change all that." Dwylah knew then what she was going to do.

Josie realized what the older woman was up to and smiled at her in delight. "That's a wonderful idea!"

"Will you help me?"

"Yes! Let me finish up my chores and we'll get started right away. It'll be good for Jack."

"Yes, it will," Dwylah agreed.

Jack was glad when he finally finished his paperwork. He was tired of sitting at his desk and wanted to get up and move around. He left the office and went out into the hall, wanting to go outside for a little while. He missed his daily rides and working with the hands. Ranching had been his life. He started past the parlor door and stopped when he saw Dwylah and Josie hard at work, decorating the mantel with strings of berries and popcorn.

"What—"

Dwylah looked over, surprised to see him standing there. They hadn't heard him come out of his office. She saw his scowl, and immediately took full blame, not wanting Josie to get into any trouble with him.

"Don't go getting mad at Josie. This was all my idea," she told him. "I thought you might want to have the place decorated for when Penny gets back. I couldn't find any Christmas trees around here, so Josie and I are just doing our best with what we've got."

Jack's expression eased, and he found himself smiling down at the chaperone. "It's a good idea, Dwylah. Penny will be glad we've done it."

"'We'?" she challenged, wanting to get him

involved with the decorating, too. She wanted him to fully experience the season this year. It was such a blessing that he and Penny had been reunited, and she wanted everything to be as perfect for them as possible.

"Well, now that I've got the book work done, I can help you, too. Wait here. I'll be right back."

Jack went upstairs to his bedroom, leaving the women behind wondering what he was up to. He returned a short time later with a box and sat down on the sofa to open it.

"What is it?" Dwylah asked, coming to sit with him.

"I used to put this out every Christmas for Penny, so she would always remember the real reason for the holiday."

He took the lid off the box and took out the carefully wrapped items inside. As he unwrapped the first item, Dwylah was delighted to see it was a wooden, hand-carved figure of Mary, and she could tell right away it was part of a manger scene.

"This is perfect. We can put it right in the middle of the mantel," she declared. "Has it been in your family for a long time?"

"I made it for Penny when she was a baby."

"This is so special," she said, carefully picking up the figurine to look at it. He had done a wonderful job carving it. "You're very talented."

"Thank you."

When Jack had all the pieces unwrapped, they

took them and arranged them prominently on the mantel.

"Now we can really decorate," Dwylah declared. "I'm glad you thought of this."

"So am I."

They shared a knowing look as they set to work, and Josie just watched and smiled.

After consulting the map again, Dan could see they were getting real close to Jack's first cache. The trail had grown narrower and more rugged, so he rode ahead of Penny to lead the way.

"Take it slow here," he called back to her.

"Don't worry. I will," she promised, more than a little on edge as she concentrated on staying in the saddle.

What happened next happened so quickly that Penny had no time to react. One moment she was making her way after Dan, and the next Ol' Midnight lost his footing, stumbled, and she was thrown.

"Dan!"

He heard her shout and reined in immediately. Panic filled him when he looked back and saw only the riderless horse on the trail behind him. He threw himself from the saddle and rushed back to look for Penny. He found her lying on the side of the trail, her eyes closed.

"Penny!"

He knelt beside her and took her into his arms.

He feared the worst, but then she opened her eyes and looked up at him.

"Dan—" Penny gazed up at him, knowing she was safe now that she was in his arms.

"Penny, are you all right?"

She lifted one hand to her head as she answered, "I think so."

"Thank God." The horror that he'd almost lost her raged through him. He took a deep breath and reminded himself that she was safe. A deep, abiding sense of relief unlike anything he'd ever felt before filled him. And suddenly he realized—

He loved her.

Dan couldn't help himself. He slowly bent to her and claimed her lips in a gentle kiss.

Penny was startled for a moment, but her surprise quickly turned to passion as she returned his kiss full measure. Dan awakened something special in her. With him, she felt completely safe, cared for . . . cherished.

With great reluctance, Dan finally made himself pull away. "Can you stand?" he asked.

What she really wanted was to stay right there in his arms, but she nodded slowly and let him help her to her feet.

Dan kept an arm around her to support her as she stood beside him, not wanting to risk her falling again. "Are you sure you're all right?"

Penny looked up at him and smiled. "As long as I'm with you—"

Mesmerized by the look in her eyes, he slowly bent to her to whisper, "I love you, Penny," as he claimed her lips in a passionate kiss.

A thrill surged through Penny at his words of love, and her breath caught in her throat. She lifted her arms to link them around his neck and draw him even closer.

Encouraged by her response, Dan crushed her to his chest and deepened the kiss. He wanted her as he had never wanted another woman.

When at last the kiss ended, Penny drew back slightly to look up at him. She saw the fierce, hungry look in his eyes and smiled gently. She lifted one hand to tenderly touch his cheek. "I love you, too, Dan."

"You do?"

She nodded, smiling up at him, her eyes aglow with all the love she felt for him.

"Oh, Penny, you have no idea how happy that makes me." He reached out to take her hand. "Come on."

"Where are we going?"

Dan drew her to him and kissed her one last time. After a long moment, he regretfully ended the embrace. "I'd much rather stay right here kissing you, but we've got to start riding again."

"I suppose you're right." She pulled away and started to move to Ol' Midnight.

"Hold up there. From now on we're going to be riding double."

"Double?"

"That's right. I've got to know you're safe, so I'm keeping you with me."

She remembered what he'd told her on the trip from St. Louis about tying her up, and she found herself smiling at him. "Well, at least, you're not going to tie me up."

"Are you planning on running away?"

"Never," she promised softly.

"Good."

Dan grabbed up Ol' Midnight's reins and then mounted his own horse. He helped Penny up behind him.

"Hold on tight. I don't want to lose you." As he said the words, he realized just how true they were. He'd lost too many people in his life. He wasn't going to lose her.

"You won't," she promised, determined never to be apart from him. She leaned close, putting her arms around his waist to help her keep her seat.

Dan urged his mount on, and, leading Ol' Midnight behind them, they continued on their trek.

A short distance behind them, John had seen everything. It seemed that pretty Penny wasn't so untouchable after all. Now he was more eager than ever to have his turn. But he couldn't let them know he was coming. Dan was too good with a gun. He'd have to take them by surprise.

Chapter Twenty

Penny kept her arms tightly around Dan's waist as they rode farther into the canyon, leading Ol' Midnight behind them.

Dan loved her and she loved him—

She couldn't believe what had just happened. His kiss had been everything she'd dreamed it would be. She couldn't wait to get back to the ranch and tell Dwylah what had happened. She smiled to herself, thinking how the chaperone would probably be immediately trying to locate the nearest justice of the peace for her. She found she liked that idea a lot.

"It should be right here," Dan said as he reined in, taking a hard look around.

Her fantasies interrupted, she slipped down off the horse's back with Dan's help and stepped back while he dismounted, too.

Dan took Jack's map out and studied it once more. He felt confident they were in the right place. With Penny following him, he made his way to the boulder Jack had drawn on the map as a clue. Following Jack's directions, he shoved aside some smaller rocks and began to dig. Penny stayed close by watching and ready to help if he needed her.

"Here!" Dan was excited and relieved when he found the small metal box buried about two feet down in the hard soil, right where Jack had indicated it would be. He lifted the box out of the hole and handed it to Penny. "Check it out and see what we've got."

Penny sat down and opened the lid to find a treasure trove of money. "Oh my! I don't believe it . . ."

Dan couldn't believe it, either, when he saw the amount of cash there. He'd known Jack was tight with his money, but he'd never dreamed the boss had managed to save up this much—and this was only one of the three hidden sites. "Don't worry about counting it right now. We can do that later tonight. Close it up and we'll go find the second box. It's only another two miles farther into the canyon."

Penny closed the box and handed it to Dan so he could stow it with their gear. She shivered a little as a cold wind gust swept through the canyon, bringing the harsh reminder that it was winter. She just happened to glance up at the sky as she was walking back to the horses with Dan.

"The sky looks strange."

Dan glanced up and and immediately knew there might be trouble. The clouds had an odd blue-gray tint. "We'd better ride fast."

Penny realized what she was seeing and knew he was right. "It's a blue norther, isn't it?"

"It looks like it. So we don't want to take any chances. We don't have a lot of time, so let's go."

They quickly mounted his horse again and rode off toward Jack's second hiding place.

John had been watching as they'd dug up the money box. He'd been waiting for the perfect moment to confront them, but before he could make his move, he overheard Dan say they were going after another box. Excited to learn there was even more money to be found, John knew he had to wait a little longer. It would definitely be worth it, especially since they would be even farther down in the canyon and that would give him more time to make his getaway. He continued to trail them, more determined than ever.

It was just what Dan had feared. The blue norther came tearing across the countryside with its harsh, freezing winds. The temperature had been cold to start with, but it quickly dropped another twenty-five degrees. Dan knew it was only a matter of time before the snow started. Wanting to have Penny in a safe, warm place before it got too bad outside, he urged his horse on to a quicker pace and covered the final miles to the second hiding place. By the time they neared the site, the snow had begun to fall.

Penny shivered, and Dan tightened his arms around her.

"If things go as easily this time as they did at

the first place, I should be able to get us to the next line shack in less than an hour."

"I never thought I'd be so excited about staying in a line shack, but right now it sounds really luxurious."

Dan remembered Jack's directions and rode to the location. It surprised him, and challenged him, to discover the place where the money was hidden was halfway down a steep incline. He knew this one was going to be harder to find, especially the way it was snowing right then. They were going to have to leave the horses tied up a distance away and make their way on foot to the location indicated on the map.

"So it's down there?" Penny said, looking down the steep, rocky hillside. In good weather it would have been difficult to reach, but in the snow, it was going to be slick and treacherous. Even so, they had no choice. The weather wouldn't be getting any better any time soon.

"If you want, you can wait here for me, and I'll go see if I can find it," Dan offered as they both dismounted.

"I'm not letting you go down there by yourself. It's too dangerous."

"That's why I want you to stay here," he told her.

Penny touched his arm and looked up at him. "We're in this together, Dan."

He was so tempted to kiss her, but he knew it was definitely not the time to even think about it, with the way the snow was coming down. "All right. Let's go, but stay right with me. I don't want you to fall."

Dan started down the incline, taking great care as he made his way among the rocks heading in the direction indicated on Jack's map.

Penny slipped several times, but managed to stay on her feet. She was impressed at how agilely Dan moved over the rocks, never wavering even in the treacherous ground. She was glad when Dan finally stopped and started to clear a place so they could begin to dig for the buried money.

"Do you think this is it?" she asked, studying the area for another clue.

"According to the map, this should be the place," he told her.

John couldn't believe his luck. Things were turning out far better than he'd ever hoped. He knew this was going to be perfect. First, he'd set their horses loose and run them off, and then he'd get the money and take off himself. His plan was perfect. This blue norther would take care of everything else for him.

Dan and Penny were so far away from any of the line shacks that they wouldn't last out in the freezing cold and heavy snow, and even if they did survive, he would be long gone by the time anyone rescued them. They'd never find him.

Feeling more confident than ever, John cautiously moved down to where they'd left their horses tied up. He was silent as he approached the horses, and he quickly looked through their saddlebags. He found the metal box he was looking for from the first dig and set it aside. Grinning broadly, he ran their horses off and then went to find them.

As John reached the drop-off on the side of the road, he was surprised to find Dan and Penny already on their way back. They were carrying another box of money. He stepped back to stay out of sight until Dan was up on the trail. Then he'd do what he needed to do to get the money and run.

Dan was helping Penny keep her footing on the treacherous hillside. The cold was numbing and the snow was coming down even harder now. He was surprised to see John there waiting for them and immediately feared the worst—that he'd come to find them because Jack had died.

"John, what happened?" Dan asked as he reached the trail and helped Penny up to stand with him.

"Nothing's happened . . . yet," John said, his tone serious.

"Then why are you here? You're supposed to be out working stock," Dan demanded.

"I'm here to get myself a raise, Dan."

"What are you talking about?"

John grew deadly serious. "I want the money." He drew his gun and aimed it directly at them. "Just toss the box over here, real easylike."

Dan was furious. The weather was hard enough to deal with, without having a fool like John show up, wanting to rob them. "Don't do this, John. You'll never get away with it."

Penny was standing right behind Dan. She was as angry as Dan was. She'd actually buckled on her gun belt that morning, and she was tempted to try to draw on the man, but it had been so long since she'd used it, she feared she wouldn't be fast enough. She waited, biding her time to see if there was anything she could do to help.

"Thieves only get in trouble if they get caught," John sneered, "and they ain't never going to catch me. I'll be so far gone before anyone finds out what I did, they won't have any idea where to start looking. Now throw that box over here, or I'll shoot the girl." John saw the anger flare in the foreman's eyes and he knew he'd struck a nerve with him. It just made him feel even more powerful and more in control. "That's right, I'll take care of Jack's daughter first if you don't co-operate. Now give me that money."

Dan had no choice. Out of fear for Penny's safety, he tossed the box toward John and it landed close beside him.

"Good, that's a start. Now throw your gun over here, Dan—real slowlike."

Dan wanted to draw and shoot. He'd had a

time a few years back when he'd been known as a fast draw, but right now he didn't want to take the risk for fear that Penny might be wounded in the shoot-out that would follow. He slowly drew his gun from his holster and tossed it a few feet in front of him.

"Now what?" Dan demanded.

"I want Penny's gun, too. I ain't blind." He looked straight at her, his expression full of hatred. "Come on, city girl. Throw the gun up here."

Penny stepped up beside Dan and did as she was ordered. "My father will catch you," she threatened.

"No, he won't, 'cause he's going to be dead," he came back at her as he kicked both their guns toward the edge of the trail. "I won't have to worry about any of you. You'll be dead, too."

Dan knew he had to do something fast. When John bent down to pick up the box, he would go after him. If he jumped him fast enough, he just might be able to overpower him.

John was keeping a careful eye on the foreman. He knew what a hard man Dan was, and he didn't trust him for a minute. "Don't even think about trying anything, Dan," he threatened. "I've got you good, right now—real good, and you know it."

John was smirking as he moved forward and cautiously bent down to pick up the cash box.

The moment John looked away, Dan launched himself at him.

John wasn't caught totally off guard. Out of the corner of his eye, he saw Dan move, and he fired blindly in his direction. The shot winged Dan in the upper arm just as Dan managed to knock him to the ground. John's gun flew from his grip.

The pain jarred Dan, but he couldn't let it stop him. With all the strength he could muster, he attacked John.

Penny was horrified as she watched the two men fighting wildly on the rocky ground. She wanted to help, and she rushed over to try to find her gun.

John cursed himself for not getting off a better shot at Dan. In a desperate move, he hit Dan's wounded arm as hard as he could. Dan gasped in pain and his grip slackened. Taking advantage of the moment, John managed to shove his opponent away and scramble to his feet.

He looked over just in time to see Penny running to get one of the discarded weapons. John threw himself at Penny and knocked her down just as she was about to grab up one of the guns. She was fighting him fiercely as he held her down on the ground. Until he could get his gun back, he'd use her as a shield.

Before John could do anything else, Dan grabbed him by the shoulder and hauled him off Penny. John savagely kicked out, knocking Dan down, and they battled again on the hard, rocky ground, rolling dangerously close to the edge of the trail.

Penny quickly scrabbled off the ground and retrieved her gun. But before she could get close enough to use it, she heard a shout. She spun around to see the two men tumble off the side of the snow-covered, icy trail. Horrified, Penny raced to the trail's edge and looked down to see them nearly halfway down the steep incline. Dan had landed on a large boulder while John was hanging on to a nearby rocky ledge, screaming.

"Help! Help me!"

"Dan! Dan, are you all right?"

"Yeah." Dan struggled to sit up, clutching his bleeding arm. He heard John's cries and carefully made his way over to see where the other man was. Dan was tempted to leave him there to fend for himself, but he knew he couldn't. Somehow, he was going to bring him back up and take him into town to turn him over to the sheriff.

"Can you get up here on your own?"

"Go get the rope off his saddle!" Dan called to her, knowing he had to try to save him.

She ran to do as he'd ordered.

"All right, toss it down here!" Dan told her when she returned.

"Toss it down to you? Don't you want me to pull you up?"

"No, I've got to try to get it down to John—"

He wanted to help John? Penny was shocked

after all that had happened, but she didn't argue.

Dan caught the rope and inched over to the rim of the boulder where John was holding on for dear life. "John! Grab the rope and I'll pull you up!"

John reached out and tried to make a grab for the rope. In an instant, though, he lost his grip on the ledge. His cry of terror echoed off the canyon walls as he fell. By Dan's reckoning, there was no way he could have survived. With a heavy heart, he pulled the rope back up and then started to climb the rocky incline. The footing was dangerous, and it was hard to get a solid hold on any of the rocks because of the snow. He moved slowly, favoring his injured arm as he cautiously climbed ever higher.

Penny stayed by the trail's edge, watching his every move and praying for his safety. Those were the longest moments of her life as she waited for Dan to make his way back to her.

Chapter Twenty-one

The moment Dan managed to climb back up onto the trail, Penny was at his side. She put an arm around him.

"How bad is your arm?" she asked.

"I've had worse," he managed to answer, his jaw locked against the pain. He could tell the gunshot wound wasn't serious, but it did need some doctoring.

"We need to bandage it. Let me take a look at it," she offered.

They went over to the horse, and Penny quickly went through John's gear looking for something they could use for a bandage. She cut some strips from the bedroll, and after seeking shelter from the freezing cold under a rocky overhang, Dan took off his coat and shirt so she could bind the wound tightly to keep it from bleeding.

"That should hold for a while," she told him as she helped him get his shirt back on.

"It feels better," Dan said as he shrugged into his coat. "Now let's ride. The other line shack isn't far."

"Thank heaven John's horse didn't run off." Penny knew they would have been in real trouble if they'd been completely stranded.

"If he had, we might not have made it back until the spring thaw."

"If at all—"

"We would have found a way to survive," he said. He had been in worse situations, and he'd survived. He would do it again, and he would make sure that Penny was safe.

Dan got his own gun and John's, while Penny found hers. They loaded up Jack's boxes and put John's gun in a saddlebag just in case they might need it. They mounted up, ready to ride to the second line shack. Dan had thought about trying to make the ride back to the first one, so they would be closer to the ranch house, but as bad as the weather was, he didn't want to risk it. This line shack was closer, and he was going to get them there as quickly as he could. Right now they just needed to wait out the bad weather.

The snow seemed to let up a little as they rode on, and he was glad. He just hoped they were already through the worst of the storm. It would make it far easier for them to find the third box and get back home.

"There it is," he told Penny as the line shack came into view.

While Dan took care of the horse, Penny carried their gear inside. Together, they brought in a load of firewood and quickly closed the door against the harsh wind and blowing snow.

Relief swept through the both of them as they

stood for a moment in silence just looking around the room.

"I was so afraid—" Penny turned to Dan, all the terror of the day's events showing in her expression as she finally realized it was over.

Dan opened his arms to her and she went to him. "It's over. You're safe now," he reassured her.

She looked up at him, seeing the strength of him in his handsome features. "Only because of you."

Penny couldn't resist. She drew him down to her and kissed him.

Dan held her close and savored the moment. He was thankful things had turned out the way they had.

When the kiss ended, they moved slightly apart.

"You're warming me up, Penny, but I think I'd better start a fire in the stove for us, too," he told her, giving her one last, gentle kiss.

Penny felt the same way. She was finding that there was nothing she loved more than being in Dan's arms. The fear that had haunted her during the showdown with John had only made her realize even more how much Dan meant to her. She stood back and watched as he quickly got the fire started. When she could feel the warmth spreading through the shack, she shed her coat.

It was starting to get dark outside, so Penny lit the one lamp that was on the table and set about seeing what food there was stored there. There wasn't much, only a few cans of beans, but she knew it was better than nothing. Penny went to look out the window and found it was snowing harder again.

Dan took off his coat and went to stand with her at the window. "I was hoping it was letting up, but it doesn't look like it. We may be here for a while."

"How long?" She was worried about her father and wanted to get back to the ranch house.

"It's hard to tell with these storms. We'll have to wait it out. There's no way we can get back to the ranch house right now."

"It is beautiful, as long as you're not out riding in it," she finished with a grin. "I wonder how Dwylah would have done if she'd been with us?"

Dan grinned, too. "Well, for sure, we wouldn't be bored right now, if she had ridden along."

Suddenly, Penny got a twinkle in her eyes as she gazed up at him. "You're bored?"

Dan bit back a groan at her teasing look and pulled her close. "Not at all."

His lips sought hers in a passionate exchange that let her know he was glad Dwylah wasn't there.

When they finally ended the kiss and moved apart, Penny asked, keeping her expression innocent this time, "Which do you like best? Being on the top or on the bottom?"

"You are a troublemaker, woman," he growled at her while he was chuckling.

"I know," she teased. "I had a good teacher." Then she grew more serious as she told him, "Right now I like the bottom. Take off your shirt and lie down. I want to take care of your arm."

Dan did as he was told. As he watched her get ready to doctor his wound, he realized he'd had some hard times in his life, but staying here alone with Penny in the line shack was going to be one of the hardest things he'd ever done. He wanted her as he'd never wanted another woman, and he reminded himself that it was his job to protect her and keep her safe. She was a challenge—that was for sure, but it was one challenge he was never going to give up on.

Penny came to sit beside the bed. She carefully removed her makeshift bandage and took a good look at the wound before beginning to wash it with the water she'd warmed on the stove.

"It doesn't look too bad," Dan said, glancing over at his arm.

"You were lucky."

"I know." He was grim as he thought of what might have happened if John had gotten off a better shot. He forced the thought away. They were here, and they were safely out of the weather.

Penny had never cleaned a gunshot wound before, but she did her best. As she was drying him off, her gaze traveled over his broad, hard-muscled chest. Forcing herself to concentrate on taking care of his injury, she bandaged his wounded arm up again with clean strips of cloth she'd cut from the sheets on one of the beds. "That should hold you."

Dan swung his long legs over the side of the bed and sat up, flexing his arm. "It feels better already."

"Good." She gave him his shirt back, regretting that they didn't have a clean one for him to wear.

Dan put his shirt on and got up to go look out the window again. The snow was still falling, and he knew they were going to be there for a while. He just hoped he could get her back to the ranch in time for her to spend Christmas with Jack.

Penny came to join him there. "What are we going to do?"

"The only thing we can do—stay here and wait."

"What do you think happened to our horses?"

"If we're lucky, they headed back to the ranch, and Jack will send some of the boys out to try to find us."

She looked at him through lowered lashes. "I hope they don't get here too soon."

Dan knew she was trouble—the kind of trouble he had come to love. "Me, too." Alone in the warmth of the line shack, he kissed her tenderly. "I love you, Penny."

She reached up to touch his cheek in a gentle caress. "I love you, too."

"Will you marry me?" he asked, knowing there would be no better time, but he was puzzled when she frowned slightly.

"Oh yes! Yes, I'll marry you!" Penny hadn't

been expecting his proposal, but she was thrilled nonetheless. She couldn't imagine spending her life with anyone else. She kissed him quickly, but then drew slightly away from him as she added, "But . . ."

He had been overwhelmed when she'd said yes, but her sudden hesitation afterward troubled him. "What? Is something wrong?" Whatever was troubling her, he would find a way to take care of it.

"It's Dwylah." She fought to keep from smiling.

"What about her?" Dan was confused. If anything, he thought the chaperone would be glad that things had worked out this way.

"Well, she's been wanting to get you to a justice of the peace for ages now. She's not going to be happy when she finds out you're marrying me."

Dan laughed and took Penny in his arms. "I'll find a way to make it up to her."

He kissed her once more and then they set about settling in for the night as the snow continued to fall. It was much later after they'd eaten their sparse dinner and had bedded down that Penny lay curled under her blanket, thinking of how blessed she was that Dan had come into her life. He was everything she'd ever dreamed of in a man, and she loved him so much.

"Dan?" She said his name softly, not sure he was still awake.

Dan was far from drifting off. He'd been lying in the top bunk, staring at the ceiling, thinking of Penny and how much he loved her. Her call surprised him, for he thought she'd already fallen asleep. "What?"

"I need you."

It was almost a whisper, but he heard it.

Dan slipped down from the upper bunk and went to her. "What's wrong?"

"Nothing's wrong. I just want you with me. We'll be warmer together," she invited, scooting over on the lower bunk.

He knew she was right. They would be warmer together—a lot warmer. He also knew lying beside her was going to test every bit of his willpower. Still, gazing down at her and seeing her innocent beauty, he couldn't resist. He got his blanket and stretched out on his side next to her. He made sure she was wrapped up in her blanket and then he spread his blanket over both of them before drawing her to him for a tender kiss.

"I'm warmer already," she told him with a grin.

"So am I," he said, gathering her close so her head rested on his shoulder. He could feel her soft body against him and tried not to think about how wonderful their wedding night was going to be. He closed his eyes, savoring the intimacy of their time alone.

Penny turned toward him and rested a hand on his chest. "I love you so much. When I think about what could have happened to you in the fight—"

Dan felt her tremble, and he kissed her softly

and pressed her head down on his shoulder, gently stroking her hair. "It's over now. We're here and we're safe—and warm," he added.

His touch and the deep sound of his voice comforted her, and she nestled even closer to him as she closed her eyes, knowing this was as close to heaven as she had ever been. "Good night . . ."

Dan pressed a kiss on her forehead as he cradled her against him. He couldn't believe everything had turned out the way it had, and he knew he was going to spend the rest of his life showing her just how much he loved her. He wanted to make love to her right then. He could think of nothing more wonderful than making her his own in all ways, but he respected her too much to take advantage of this time they had together. He would get them back to the ranch house as quickly as he could, so he could ask Jack for his permission to marry his daughter. He wanted to do things the proper way. Penny deserved that much.

Dan didn't fall asleep right away. Her nearness and the harsh sound of the wind outside kept him awake for quite a while. He hoped the storm would clear out by morning, but he knew it didn't sound good. At least, they were safe for now. He would get Penny back to Jack at the ranch, and he would get her to the altar just as quickly as he could after that. He smiled at the thought that he would have a family again, and he knew that would be the best Christmas present he'd ever received.

Dan awoke early the next morning and looked over at Penny, where she was still sleeping close beside him. He took the time to study her, thinking she was the most beautiful woman he'd ever seen. He carefully managed to slip out of the bunk, taking care not to disturb her, and went to look out the window. He'd been hoping that the weather had cleared overnight, but the sight that greeted him wasn't what he'd hoped for. The snow was still coming down so heavily he could barely see more than a foot out the window. Frustrated, but knowing there was nothing he could do about it, he accepted his fate.

For now he was trapped with Penny in the line shack.

At any other time, he would have been perfectly happy to stay there alone with her, but his concern about the state of Jack's health left him tense. Knowing there was little he could do right then, he made up his mind to bide his time and wait for the opportunity to ride out as soon as they could.

Chapter Twenty-two

It was late that afternoon when Dwylah was sitting in the parlor reading. The snowfall had let up earlier in the day and things had been quiet around the ranch. She was startled when she heard some shouting outside, and she got up from the sofa to see what all the excitement was about. It seemed a bit early for Danny and Penny to be back. Jack had told her they would be gone for at least four or five days, but then since the weather had turned bad with the snow, she thought they might have decided to return to the ranch house early.

Dwylah was eager to see them. Things were definitely too quiet around there without Danny. Looking out, she spotted some of the ranch hands down by the stable, but she had no idea what they seemed to be so excited about. It wasn't long before she saw one of them running up to the house. The fact that he was running frightened her. She rushed out into the hallway to call for Jack, who was upstairs resting.

"Jack! Get down here!"

Jack had been half asleep when he heard her call, and he knew it had to be important if Dwylah was calling him. He managed to get up out of bed and start from the bedroom to see what was wrong. When he reached the top of the stairs, he saw Lou in the front hall with Dwylah. Jack hurried down the steps as fast as he could go.

"What is it?" he asked, seeing Lou's worried expression.

"We got trouble, Jack," he told him. "Dan and Penny's horses just came back without them."

"What?" Dwylah reacted first, horrified.

Jack was somber. "When?"

"Just a few minutes ago. We checked them over to see if they'd been injured in any way, but the horses seem fine."

"But Penny and Dan—" Jack was frowning as he tried to figure out what had happened to them.

"No sign of them," Lou said, his tone somber.

"This isn't like Dan."

"Not at all. That's why I already told Fred to saddle up our horses, so we can ride out while it's still daylight. Where did they ride to?"

"Up to the north side of the canyon," Jack said.

"All right. We'll get some supplies and head out in the next few minutes."

"Do you think you can reach the first line shack before nightfall?" He worried about Lou and Fred being out in this weather, too.

"We're going to try," Lou promised.

"I wish I could ride with you," he said solemnly.

"I wish you could, too. You're the best tracker

on the Lazy Ace," Lou said as he started back toward the door.

"Lou—"

The ranch hand looked back to see what his boss wanted.

"Find them."

The look in Jack's eyes told him all he needed to know. "I won't come back without them."

After spending an entire day snowed in at the line shack worrying about how he was going to get Penny back to her father, Dan went out to take a look around. There was no way they were going to be able to go after the money Jack had hidden at the third spot, so he wanted to return to the house as soon as possible. They could find the rest of the money later, when the weather got better.

Dan checked on the horse first and then walked farther out away from the shack to see how bad the trail was. Riding double on the way up the canyon in good weather had been one thing, but they were going to have to be extra cautious in the snow. As he made his way closer to the trail, he saw something up in one of the trees and smiled, knowing he was going to take some of that back to the shack with him.

Penny had realized how restless Dan was when he went outside, and since they were going to be there at least until the following morning, she decided to make this evening a very special one for him.

Tonight, she was going to surprise him.

They were going to celebrate their engagement with a romantic candlelight dinner. She'd found a candle in one of the drawers earlier, and while he was gone, she was going to do her best to make this a banquet he wouldn't forget. She put the candle in a candleholder in the middle of the table for their decorative centerpiece. She wished she'd had some decorations to put up, too, but this was a line shack, after all.

Penny was smiling as she put the beans on the top of the stove to heat up and then set the table with the "fine china." The metal plates were going to have to do. She wished they had a bottle of wine so they could make a toast, but they would have to be satisfied drinking water. Her engagement banquet might not prove to be the social event of the season, but it was going to be a wonderful night for the two of them.

Thoughts of an "engagement banquet" made her think of her mother, and she grew sad for a moment. She had never known why her parents' marriage hadn't worked out, but she was determined that her marriage to Dan was going to last. She was going to do everything in her power to make sure they lived happily ever after.

Penny went to look out the window and saw that he was on his way back. She quickly lit the candle and put the pot of beans on the table. She stood back to watch him as he came through the door.

Dan was carrying his present for Penny behind him as he came back into the line shack. It was the closest thing to bringing her flowers as he could find, stranded as they were. When he walked in the door, though, his idea of surprising her was lost as she surprised him. There before him was what looked to be a romantic dinner. There was a lighted candle on the table, their places were set, and the pot of beans was waiting for them. Penny was standing behind the table, bathed in the candlelight, looking more beautiful than ever.

"I wanted to surprise you," she said.

"You did," he answered, quickly shutting the door. He went to her and held out his gift. "Here. I brought you some mistletoe."

Penny's eyes widened in surprise. She'd never seen it grown in the wild this way. "Where did you find it?"

"It grows on the trees out here."

"I'm glad. I was looking for something to decorate with," she said as she took it from him, and then stood on tiptoes to give him a quick kiss. "But you didn't really need the mistletoe to get a kiss, you know." She gave him a flirtatious look.

He grabbed her and pulled her to him, seeking her lips in a hungry exchange that left her heart racing when they finally moved apart.

Penny gazed up at him, wondering what it was going to be like on their wedding night. She had no idea what really went on between a man and a woman, but after kissing Dan these last few days and snuggling up with him in her bunk last night, she was growing more and more eager to find out. "We'd better eat."

"All right," he agreed, somewhat reluctantly. What he really wanted to do was pick her up in his arms and carry her off to one of the lower bunks.

While he took off his coat and washed his hands, Penny decorated the table with the mistletoe. When he wasn't looking, she hid a piece of the mistletoe in a strategic place to surprise him with later. Stepping back, she admired their fancy dinner.

"Let's eat," Dan said, coming back to give her one more kiss. This time it was a sweet one, for he didn't want to tempt himself any more than he already had.

They sat down at the table and said grace before Penny passed him the dish of beans.

"I hope you like my cooking," she said with a grin.

"It smells delicious," he countered.

They were both smiling as they served themselves.

"This wasn't quite the banquet I always dreamed of—" she began.

"I'm sorry," Dan put in, knowing how rough this had to be for her.

"Don't you dare apologize, Dan Roland. You didn't let me finish. I was going to say that while it's not what I always dreamed of, it's even better. Just the two of us, here, celebrating." Penny picked up her glass of water and held it out to Dan. "To our engagement."

He lifted his glass and touched it to hers. "To us," he told her, and they both took a drink.

They enjoyed their meal, knowing under the circumstances that they were very blessed to have a roof over their heads, a warm place to sleep, and something hot to eat.

"How bad was it outside?" Penny asked as they finished eating.

"We should be able to start back in the morning. It'll be a hard ride, but if the weather holds we should be able to make it at least to the other line shack tomorrow."

"I wonder if our horses made it back to the house."

"If they did, I'm sure your father sent some of the boys out to look for us."

"The sooner we get back, the better."

Penny got up from the table to clean up after their dinner, but Dan had other ideas. As she started past him, he caught her arm and pulled her down on his lap.

"I love you, Penny," he said.

Their gazes met, and time stood still. Slowly, he bent to her and kissed her. It started off as a sweet kiss, but the feel of her against him lit a fire within Dan and he scooped her up in his arms as he stood up and carried her over to one of the lower bunks. Ever so gently, he laid her down on the bed and then he joined her there, taking her in his arms again.

Penny felt the heat of his body next to hers and wrapped her arms around him. She wanted to be as close to him as she could be, and when he moved over her, she thrilled to his nearness. His lips found hers, and she shivered in delight. She had never been so intimate with a man before, but she was enjoying it. Innocent that she was, she had no idea how her restless movements aroused Dan even more, and she was devastated when he broke off the kiss and shifted slightly away from her.

"Dan . . . ?" Penny whispered, wanting to be back in his arms kissing him. When she heard him give a half groan, half chuckle, she grew even more confused, and when he sat up on the side of the bunk, she was hurt. "Why did you stop?"

Dan glanced over his shoulder at her and saw her innocent confusion. He turned back and kissed her softly. "I had to, Penny. If I hadn't stopped right then, I wouldn't have been able to stop at all. I want to save our lovemaking for our wedding night."

"Oh—" She suddenly realized what he was talking about and she blushed. "Can we go find a justice of the peace right now?"

"Believe me, if there was one nearby, we'd be on our way. I love you, girl."

"I love you, too."

Dan got up and Penny followed. As he started to go add more wood to the stove, she stopped him.

"There is one thing you missed—"

"What?"

"I get another kiss—" She pointed to where she'd put the small piece of mistletoe in the upper bunk.

"I think I can be forced to oblige you." Dan laughed and took her in his arms for one last passionate embrace before setting her from him. "I'm real glad I brought that mistletoe back for you."

"So am I," she agreed. "I may just keep a piece of it with me all the time now."

"I think that's a real good idea."

He helped her clean up after the dinner and they began to make their plans for riding out early in the morning. Dan wanted to cover as many miles as they could the following day.

When they bedded down for the night, Dan took Penny in his arms again and held her close, kissing her one last time before trying to sleep. As they lay together, both were regretting that there wasn't a justice of the peace anywhere nearby.

Chapter Twenty-three

It was midafternoon the following day as the stagecoach made its run into Sagebrush. Lacey's mood was strained. Soon their trip would be over. Soon she would be separated from little Steve and the reverend, and she would probably never see them again. The possibility broke her heart. She had never known a man as kind and gentle as Nick, and she loved Steve dearly. She hadn't had the chance to talk with Nick privately about Steve yet, but if she'd had a way to support herself, she would have asked to adopt the boy right then and there. As unsettled as her life was, she had nothing to offer him. She didn't know how she was going to feed herself, let alone take care of a young boy, too.

Lacey glanced over at the reverend and saw the tension and excitement in his expression. Soon he would know where his brother had gone—or, at least, she hoped he would find out, and then they would be reunited. She wished she could be there with him when they came face-to-face for the first time after all these years. She knew it was going to be a wonderful, life-changing moment they would never forget.

* * *

Nick couldn't remember the last time he'd been this excited. Danny was somewhere nearby and he was going to find him.

"It won't be long now," Steve said, seeing the look on his face.

"I know. I just wonder how hard it will be to track him down in town."

"Don't worry. We'll do it. We didn't come all this way to lose him now," Steve said.

"This was your idea, you know." Nick smiled down at him. "I wouldn't be here if it hadn't been for you."

Steve looked very proud at his compliment, and he told him earnestly, "We're gonna find him. We're gonna find him today!"

"We wish you luck, Reverend," the other folks in the stagecoach told him.

"Thank you."

Steve felt the stagecoach slowing down a bit, so he unfastened the covering over the window and got his first look at the main street of Sagebrush. "We're here!"

The stage rolled to a stop, and the driver jumped down and opened the door for them. Nick climbed out and then helped Lacey descend and Steve get down. The snow had been cleared away from the depot.

"The hotel's right down the street, folks," the driver announced as he got their bags down for them.

Lacey wasn't quite sure what to do. She had

very little money and had to find a job real quick. "I guess I'll be seeing you around," she said to Nick and Steve. She turned away and started to move off.

Steve wasn't about to let her go that easily. "Where are you going?"

"I thought I'd see how much a room costs at the hotel," she began.

"That's where we're going," Steve said. "Let's all go together."

Lacey looked up at the reverend, unsure how he would react. It had been one thing being nice to her on the stage. It was another, now that they were in town.

"You're right, Steve. We should go together." He met her gaze. "And after we've checked in, we're going to pay a visit at the general store. If you're going to start your new life here, you're going to need a dress of some kind."

She was shocked. No one ever took care of her. "I'll be fine."

"Yes, you will be. We're going to give you an early Christmas present. Steve and I are going to pay for your hotel room and get you a new dress."

"But, Reverend—" she protested, embarrassed.

"You can't turn down a Christmas present," Steve scolded her, grabbing up his own bag. "C'mon. Let's go. I'm cold."

"I think we need to go," Nick said wryly.

"I think you're right," she agreed.

They made their way to the hotel and were

glad to enter the welcoming warmth of the lobby. The clerk had seen the stage pull in and he'd been waiting to see if anyone was coming to take a room.

"Afternoon, folks," the clerk greeted them. "You be needing a room?" He thought they were a family.

Nick spoke up. "Actually, we need two rooms. One for Miss McCormick and one for us."

"All right," he said, pushing the book across the counter so they could register. Once they'd signed in, he looked at their names. "Welcome to Sagebrush, Reverend Miller—and Steve." He nodded to the girl, who he thought was dressed rather oddly in pants, but it wasn't his business what she wore as long as they paid him. He quickly quoted the price and was pleased when the reverend handed over the money. "Thanks, Reverend." He gave him the keys. "Rooms ten and twelve at the top of the steps and to your right."

"Thank you. There is one thing I wanted to ask you—" Nick began. He had no idea if the clerk was familiar with everyone in town, but it didn't hurt to ask after coming all this way.

"How can I help you?" The clerk was earnest in his offer.

"I'm trying to find my brother, and I have reason to believe he's here in Sagebrush."

The clerk frowned. "I don't know anyone else by the name of Miller, Reverend. Sorry."

"No, his name's not Miller. His name is Danny Roland."

"Dan?" The clerk was surprised that they had different names, but he didn't say anything. "Why, Dan is Jack Anderson's foreman out at the Lazy Ace."

"He's really here?" After all this time, Nick could scarcely believe it.

"Yes, he is. Of course, getting out to the Lazy Ace ain't gonna be easy for you with the snow, but one of the boys down at the stable should be able to drive you out there."

"Thank you! Is it very far out to the ranch?"

"It's a good ride. You're better off waiting until tomorrow morning. The traveling might be a little easier."

"I appreciate your help."

Lacey looked at the reverend as they made their way up the stairs. "Your prayers have been answered."

He looked over at her. "I can't believe it. I don't think this will seem real until I actually get to see him again."

"I hope everything goes well for you," Lacey told him.

"Thank you." He was sincere. "Why don't we get cleaned up and then go over to the general store? Since we're not leaving for the Anderson Ranch until tomorrow, we can get you a dress and then have dinner."

"Are you sure?" Lacey was hesitant. She worried about him being seen in public with her. It had been one thing riding on the stagecoach together, but here in Sagebrush, she knew people would talk.

"Of course. Now hurry up. We don't know what time the store is going to close today."

"I'll be ready in a few minutes."

Nick and Steve saw her into her own room before going on to theirs.

"What do you think it's going to be like going out to a real ranch?" Steve asked, eager and excited about the day to come.

"I don't know, but we're going to find out," Nick answered. He paused and smiled at the boy. "Thank you for making this trip with me, Steve."

Steve beamed up at him. "Just think—if we hadn't come here to find your brother, we would never have met Miss Lacey."

"She's a special young woman."

"Yes, she is," Steve agreed. He had never told the reverend about the night at the way station when Miss Lacey had come to him and helped him.

"All right, wash up, so we can go," Nick directed.

Steve took off his coat and hurried to the washstand, while Nick took off his coat and sat down on the side of the bed to wait his own turn.

In her room, Lacey had quickly shed her coat to get freshened up. Reverend Miller had proven himself to truly be a man of God. She couldn't believe how kind he'd been and how generous. She'd been blessed to have him come into her life. He didn't have to pay for her room or buy her any clothes, and yet he wouldn't take no for an answer. He told her they were early presents, yet she had nothing to give him. She was going to be lucky to have enough money to buy Steve some candy for Christmas.

Lacey didn't let her thoughts linger on the bad things. The past was over and she was starting a whole new life. Reverend Miller and Steve had helped her in so many ways. The reverend's true kindness and the boy's innocent love were amazing. She felt more confident in herself now that she'd spent time with them. She'd never known anyone like them before, and it hurt her to think that her time with them was nearly at an end. She put that thought from her, though, for she wanted to enjoy every moment they had left.

A short time later, Nick and Steve came for Lacey and they left the hotel, heading for the general store. The lady at the counter was helpful and picked out a suitable demure day gown for Lacey to try on. Nick and Steve wandered about the store while she went in the back to put it on.

Lacey undressed in the back room and donned the long-sleeved, high-necked day gown. It had been so long since she'd worn a dress like this one that she wasn't quite sure how she looked.

"What do you think?" Lacey asked as she went out to find them.

"You look real pretty, Miss Lacey!" Steve said adoringly.

Nick had known she was pretty. In her dance hall gown, she'd been really sexy, but now, seeing her dressed like a lady, he thought she was the loveliest woman he'd ever seen. "Yes, you do," he agreed with Steve.

She actually blushed at their compliments. "Well, thanks."

"She'll take it," Nick told the clerk.

Lacey was still wearing her boots, but that didn't matter. It wasn't like she was going dancing anywhere, and they were practical in the snow.

"And she'll need a pair of shoes, too," Nick added.

She started to object, but the look he gave her stopped her.

"Merry Christmas, Lacey."

The clerk quickly helped her choose a pair of comfortable shoes, and they were ready to leave. Because of the snow, she put her boots on for the walk back to the hotel. They stopped at the stable so Nick could arrange their ride to the ranch in the morning. When they reached the hotel, Lacey took the bag with her old clothes in it up to her room, and then they went into the small dining room to have dinner.

As accustomed as they were to the tight quarters of the way stations, the hotel dining room seemed quite spacious and elegant, and they found the food was delicious.

"I can't wait to get out to the ranch and see your brother," Steve said, excitement growing within him.

"I feel the same way," Nick agreed.

"I'm so happy for you," Lacey told him, smiling at him across the table.

"This has been an adventure, that's for sure."

They talked over dinner how she was going to look for a job in town the next day, and when they'd finished eating they went back upstairs. They stopped outside Lacey's room to say good night.

"I hope everything goes well for you tomorrow," Lacey told the reverend.

"Thank you, and I hope you find a job," he said.

"So do I. Keep that in your prayers."

"We will," Nick promised. "We'll come back and see you when we're in town."

"I'd like that." She looked down at Steve and then bent down to give him a hug. "You take care of Reverend Miller."

"I will."

"Good boy."

They were smiling as she went into her room and closed the door.

Lacey stood just inside her room and fought back the tears that threatened at the thought that she wouldn't be seeing much of them anymore. Realizing she had to be strong, she tried to be optimistic. She had escaped from Phil and the horrible life she'd been living. She was in a new town, starting over. Things could only get better. As she went to bed that night, she said a prayer for the reverend that the reunion with his brother would go well, and she prayed for help finding a job so she could live a better life.

Chapter Twenty-four

Nick and Steve were up early. Steve kept watch for Lacey but didn't see her that morning. After eating a quick breakfast in the hotel dining room, they hurried down to the stable to find Rob, the stable hand, ready and waiting to take them to the Lazy Ace. They climbed up onto the buckboard's driver's bench with the driver and held on as best they could as they started out on what would be one of the longest journeys in Nick's life.

"What business you got out at the Lazy Ace?" Rob asked.

"My brother, Dan Roland, is the foreman there."

"I know Dan. He's a good man."

They fell quiet then as they continued the trip out to the ranch. It was a sunny day, but still cold. They could tell it was going to be a white Christmas this year.

"There's the ranch up ahead," Rob told them as the house and outbuildings came into view.

"It looks very successful," Nick said, impressed.

"One of the best in the area. Jack Anderson's worked hard to make it what it is today."

As they pulled up in front of the house, Nick saw an older man open the front door.

"There's Jack now," the stable hand said. Then he called out, "How you doin', Jack?"

"I'm getting along all right."

"I brought you some company."

"I see that." Jack stepped out on the porch, wondering who the man with the young boy was.

Nick and Steve climbed down from the buckboard and looked quickly around, hoping to see Dan. When they saw no trace of him, they started up to the porch to speak with the ranch owner.

"Do you want me to wait for you?" Rob asked.

"If you don't mind."

Jack had heard them, and he called out, "Come on inside, too. I don't want you freezing out here while we're talking."

"I'll just go on down to the stable and visit with some of the boys."

"All right."

Jack turned his attention to the young man coming up the porch steps and he frowned. Something about him seemed familiar. "Do I know you? Who are you?"

"No, sir. We've never met before. My name's Nick Miller. I'm here to see your foreman, Danny Roland. I'm his brother."

Jack's expression changed dramatically. Dan had told him when he'd first come to work for him about how he'd been separated from a younger brother in his childhood, and the thought that his brother had found him after all this time left Jack amazed. "You're Dan's brother?"

"Yes, sir. I am."

He put out his hand to shake hands with him. "Welcome to the Lazy Ace, Nick, and who is this, your son?"

"This is Steve. He's one of the boys from the orphanage that I run."

Jack looked at Dan's brother with even greater respect. "It's nice to meet you, Steve," Jack said, shaking hands with the boy, too. "Come on in!"

Dwylah had been upstairs when she heard the buckboard drive up. She was just coming down the stairs as Jack ushered a man and a boy inside.

"Well, who do we have here?" she asked as she reached the bottom of the steps. In that moment, the man looked her way and, at her first glimpse of him, she went still. He looked so much like Danny.

"This is Nick Miller. He's Dan's brother—"

"Oh my." Dwylah couldn't believe it. Here, Dan and Penny were missing and maybe in danger and his brother had shown up. "Well, hello. I'm Dwylah, and it's so wonderful that you're here and just in time for Christmas—"

"I'm glad to be here, too."

"Dan told us about you."

"He did?" Nick was surprised.

"Yes, he did. You two went through some hard times as children."

"Yes, we did," he agreed. "And speaking of children, this is Steve."

"It's nice to meet you, Steve." She turned to the boy.

Nick glanced around the front hall. "Where is Dan? Is he around?"

Jack stepped up, his mood turning serious. "We need to talk."

"What's wrong?" Nick was suddenly worried by the change in his manner.

"Leave your coats out here and let's go in the parlor."

Nick helped Steve take his coat off and after they'd hung them up, they all made their way to sit in the parlor.

Steve's face lit up when he saw all the Christmas decorations on the mantel over the fireplace. "It's so pretty."

"Why, thank you, Steve," Jack said. "Miss Dwylah and I worked on decorating for quite a while."

"Mr. Anderson, is Dan in some kind of trouble?" Nick asked, sensing something was wrong.

"We don't know for sure," Jack began, and then he quickly told him how Dan and Penny had ridden up to the canyon, and how the storm had passed through and their horses had come back without them. "Two of my men are out searching for them right now."

"How long has it been?" Dread filled Nick. The

thought that after traveling all this way, he might have lost Danny again tormented him.

"The hands rode out the night before last, right after the horses showed up."

"Would it help if I rode out, too?" Nick offered. "I'd be glad to help with the search." He certainly knew how hard his brother could be to find if he didn't want to be found.

"Lou and Fred are my two best trackers. If anybody's going to find my daughter and Dan, it will be them."

Everyone was silent for a moment.

"So if Lou and Fred are looking for them, they'll be back real soon, right?" Steve asked in his innocence. "It is almost Christmas. They have to be back by then."

Dwylah smiled down at him tenderly, wanting to reassure him. "Yes, Steve. They'll be here."

"Good," Steve said brightly. "Reverend Miller has been waiting for this for a long time."

Dwylah and Jack both looked at Dan's brother with renewed respect.

"You're a minister?" she asked.

"Yes, ma'am. As I told Mr. Anderson, I run an orphanage in St. Louis."

"That's such a wonderful calling for you," Dwylah said.

"Yes, ma'am. It is. I get to be with children like Steve."

"So tell me, how did you find out that Dan was working here at the Lazy Ace? The two of you have been separated for so long, I'm sure Dan never thought you'd see each other again," Jack said.

Nick went on to explain what had happened at the train depot that fateful day back in St. Louis. "If it hadn't been for Steve, here, running away from the orphanage, I would never have been at the train depot and seen Danny just as he was boarding the train."

Dwylah was awestruck at his story. She looked down at the young boy, concerned about him. "Why did you run away from Reverend Miller's orphanage, Steve?"

Steve hung his head in shame.

"It's all right, Steve," Nick said.

He looked up at the elderly lady and told her how this was his first Christmas without his family, and how he'd been so scared and angry over being all by himself.

"Oh, darling, I am so glad Reverend Miller found you. Why, if he hadn't, you wouldn't be here with me right now!" she chuckled, wanting to cheer him if she could.

Her words did manage to get a shy, little smile out of him.

Dwylah glanced over at Jack then, wanting to make everyone feel better. "Well, those two hands had just better hurry up and find Penny and Danny and get them back here, don't you think, Jack?"

Jack's mood lightened in the face of her unfailing

good nature. "That's right." He looked to Nick and Steve again. "Where are you staying?"

"We have a room at the hotel in town," Nick answered.

"Why don't you go back into town and get your things and come out here and stay? We've got plenty of room, and then you'll be here when they do get back."

Nick was touched by his generosity. They were virtual strangers and yet he was opening his home to them. "We'd like that very much."

"We'd like it, too," Dwylah added.

"I'll have one of the boys follow you into town and bring you back after you get your things from the hotel," Jack said.

"Would you like to stay here with us while the reverend goes to town, Steve?" Dwylah asked, wanting to spend more time with him.

"Oh no, ma'am. I can't do that. I've got to see Miss Lacey again," he said seriously.

"Who's Miss Lacey?" Dwylah asked them both, surprised by his answer.

"She's my friend," Steve replied before Nick could say anything. "She's all alone, so I've got to go see her. She doesn't know anybody in town, and it's almost Christmas."

"Lacey came in on the stage with us," Nick explained.

Dwylah could tell this girl named Lacey meant a lot to the boy. She couldn't help herself. In her usual way, she put Jack on the spot. "Jack," she said, "have we got room enough for one more person to stay with us?"

Jack was surprised by her question, but after getting to knowing Dwylah during the time they'd been together, he knew he shouldn't have been. "I suppose we can arrange something."

"Good." She turned to Steve again. "When you get back into town, you ask your friend if she'd like to come and spend Christmas here at the ranch with us. There's no reason for her to be there in Sagebrush all by herself." Dwylah would never forget the look of delight on the boy's face at her invitation.

"Really?"

"Really. As long as that's all right with the reverend." Dwylah realized she should have included him in making the decision.

Nick didn't know how it had happened, but he found he was rather glad that Lacey wouldn't be alone this year on Christmas. He just hoped Dan got back in time to share the blessed day with them. Thinking of his brother then and knowing the potential danger he and the rancher's daughter might be in, he offered up a silent prayer for their safety and their return home.

"I'm getting worried," Lou told Fred as they covered the endless miles looking for Penny and Dan.

"They're out here somewhere. Dan's a survivor. You know that, and he's not about to let anything happen to Penny."

"But they're on foot."

That realization troubled them both deeply, for there weren't a lot of places to seek shelter here in the canyon.

Lou and Fred reined in to stare out across the snow-covered landscape, hoping to see something, anything, that would give them a clue as to where Dan and Penny were. They'd made it to the closest line shack the day before, after camping out that first night. It had been a harsh night in the cold, but they'd done it. When they reached the shack and found no sign of them, they'd immediately started out again. The traveling was slow, but they were not about to give up.

They couldn't give up.

This was Dan and Penny.

"Lou, look!" Fred almost shouted as he caught sight of the solitary horse that had just come into view in the distance with what looked like two riders on its back.

"Well, I'll be . . ." Lou couldn't believe his eyes.

"Let's go get 'em!"

They wanted to gallop over to them, but they knew better. Urging their mounts on to the safest, quickest pace, they rode out to meet them.

Dan and Penny had been riding since first light. The going was slow, but they were covering miles back toward the ranch house, and they knew that was good. It was Dan who spotted the two riders coming their way, and his mood lightened considerably.

"We've got company," he told Penny.

"Really?"

"It's Lou and Fred." Dan knew if Jack was going to send anyone out to look for them, it would have been these two.

"What are you two doing out here?" Dan asked as the two groups met. "Did you get lost in the storm?"

"I don't think we're the ones who are lost," Fred came back at him. "Are you all right, Penny?"

"I'm fine, Fred. Dan took real good care of me," she answered. "Is Papa worried?"

"I think that's safe to say," Lou said.

"Is he doing all right?" Dan asked.

"Except for worrying about Penny, here, he was fine when we left."

"Good." Dan was relieved to hear that the rancher hadn't worsened.

Just then Fred asked, "How did you end up on John's horse? Where's John?"

Dan answered cryptically, "I'll tell you on the ride back."

With that kind of answer, Fred and Lou understood that something bad had happened.

"Let's go home," Penny said. "If we're lucky, we can still make it back in time for Christmas Eve."

"If we're running too late, maybe Santa will

find us and give us a ride in his sleigh," Fred joked as they started for home.

"It would probably be warmer," Penny chimed in.

"No doubt about that," Dan agreed.

As they rode for the ranch house and Dan told them about John's ambush and attempted robbery, Penny held on to him even more tightly. The memory of how close she'd come to losing him still had the power to frighten her. She wanted to keep him near to her and never let him go.

Lacey had had a feeling things might not go easily in Sagebrush, but she figured she could handle whatever life threw her way. After spending the entire day trying to find decent employment and being turned down repeatedly, she was devastated as she returned to the hotel. She kept her expression pleasant as she passed through the lobby on her way up to her room, but once she'd gone inside, she'd locked the door behind her and thrown herself across the bed to cry her heart out.

In two more days she would be completely out of money, and she couldn't bear the thought that she would have to go back to working in a saloon just to have a bed to sleep in and food to eat. She had no idea what the future held for her now. With all the praying she'd done lately since she'd been with Reverend Miller and Steve, she wondered why her prayers hadn't been answered.

Didn't Jesus always go after those who needed his help the most? Didn't he always search for the lost sheep to save them?

The knock at the door startled her. Wiping the tears from her cheeks, she struggled to sit up and called out, "Who is it?"

"It's Steve! Open up!"

A surge of joy went through her. Steve was truly a sweet and gentle little boy, and she did love him. She was glad that she'd taken the time to buy him several pieces of candy for Christmas. If nothing else, she was going to help him keep his belief in the beauty and the goodness of the season.

"What is it, Steve?" she called out again, wanting to stall as long as she could so he wouldn't be able to tell she'd been crying. But one quick look in the small mirror over the washstand told her there was no point in trying to hide it. Her face was red and her eyes slightly swollen from the torrent of tears that had consumed her. She went to the door and opened it to find him standing there smiling at her with the reverend right beside him.

"Miss Lacey, what's the matter?" Steve didn't like knowing she'd been crying and he wanted to help her in any way he could. He knew if she stayed with them, she wouldn't be crying anymore. He'd see to it.

"Nothing. Nothing's the matter. What did you need, Steve?" She tried to ignore Reverend Miller's presence.

"We have a surprise for you. You get to spend Christmas with us!"

"What?"

"Do you mind if we come in?" Nick asked.

She stepped back and closed the door behind them.

Nick quickly explained how Jack's daughter, Penny, and Dan were missing and how they were going to stay out at the ranch with Jack to await their return.

"I'm sorry about your brother and Jack's daughter. Do you think they're safe?"

"We hope so." He went on, "Steve mentioned to Jack that you were here alone, and Jack said there's plenty of room at the ranch if you'd like to come and stay with us over Christmas."

"You want me to go with you?"

Nick gazed down at her, knowing Steve had been right. They did need her with them for Christmas. "Yes, I do want you to go with us," he said. "Pack up your things. The driver's waiting for us out in front."

"I don't have a lot to worry about," Lacey said as she donned her coat and grabbed up the one bag that contained all her worldly belongings.

As she left the hotel with Steve and the reverend to make the trip out to the ranch, Lacey understood that her prayers truly had been answered. Deeply thankful, her heart filled with joy, she offered up another prayer for the safe return of Nick's brother and the rancher's daughter.

*   *   *

Jack went upstairs to rest. He was trying to keep from being consumed by his worries about Penny and Dan, but it seemed he was fighting a losing battle, even with Dwylah around as a distraction.

Dwylah stayed in the parlor eagerly awaiting Nick and Steve's return from their trip to town. She wasn't sure who this young woman named "Lacey" was, but she knew she had to be special if the little boy adored her so much. Dwylah found out she was right when she heard the buckboard pull up out in front of the house and she hurried to let them in.

"Miss Dwylah, this is Miss Lacey," Steve said, the moment she opened the door. "Miss Lacey, this is Miss Dwylah."

Dwylah found herself staring at a remarkably lovely young woman. "It's a pleasure to meet you, Lacey. Come in."

"Thank you, Miss Dwylah," Lacey said, entering the house followed by Steve and the reverend.

"There's no need for you to call me 'Miss.' I'm just Dwylah to my friends," she laughed.

Lacey was completely taken with her from the first and she found herself smiling back at her. "Dwylah, Steve was telling me about you."

"Good things, I hope."

"What else could there be?"

"I think I like you a lot already, Lacey. Go ahead and leave your things here in the hall. Make yourselves comfortable in the parlor while I go get Jack."

She hurried upstairs to find he was just coming out of his room.

"I heard all the commotion, so I take it they're back?"

"They're downstairs waiting for you," she answered.

Together, they went down to the parlor to spend the day with them as they awaited Penny and Dan's return.

Chapter Twenty-five

It was Christmas Eve—and it was getting late—well after dark. Dwylah had excused herself and gone up to her room for a few moments. She was trying to put up a brave front, but with each passing minute, her hopes for Dan and Penny's return grew dimmer. Her heart ached as the fear that she'd tried to ignore all this time came back to haunt her.

What if something terrible had happened to them?

What would they do?

Unable to face the possibility, she forced the thoughts away.

Everything was going to be all right.

It had to be.

Penny didn't think she'd ever seen anything as beautiful as the ranch house lit up as it was in the night, far up ahead of them as they rode back in. They'd considered stopping earlier and riding back in, in the morning, but they'd all decided they would risk covering the final miles to the ranch that night. It was Christmas Eve, and Penny wanted to be with her father on what might be their last Christmas together.

"We're home," she said softly, a deep abiding love for the place filling her.

"Yes, we are," Dan agreed. He put his heels to the horse's side and they moved more quickly over the final distance to the house.

"Jack's going to be real glad to see you two tonight," Fred remarked.

"And we're going to be real glad to see him," Penny responded.

Dwylah was just about ready to go back downstairs. She paused to take one last look out at the snow-covered, moonlit night, and she was completely shocked to see three horses charging back up to the house. Excitement filled her and she ran out into the hallway.

"Jack! Jack! Somebody's riding in!" she shouted as she rushed down the steps.

Jack had been in the parlor with Nick, Lacey, and Steve, and he got up as quickly as he could to hurry from the room. He reached the front hall at the same time Dwylah made it to the bottom of the stairs. She could tell no one was going to get in his way, so she stayed back as Jack all but ran toward the front door.

But he didn't get the chance to open it, for it flew open and Penny came running into the house.

"Papa! Papa, we're home!"

Jack grabbed his girl and gave her a huge hug. If he'd been stronger he would have swung her around the hall. "Oh, Penny—we've been so worried!"

When he finally stood still, he just hugged her for a moment longer before letting her go.

It was then that Penny looked up to see the three strangers standing in the parlor doorway watching them. She frowned and started to ask who they were, just as Dan came inside carrying Jack's boxes.

"I'm so sorry, Jack," he began as he put the boxes on the small table nearby.

Dwylah immediately ran to him and pulled him down to her for a kiss on the cheek.

"All that matters is you're safe, Danny, and—" she whispered to him, but as soon as she said it she saw the bullet hole in his coat and the bloodstain. "What happened?"

Jack looked over, too, but Dan quickly told them, "It's just a scratch. I'll tell you what happened later."

Jack nodded, understanding now that something had happened to them out there, and he fully intended to find out what it was.

"Well, this will make you feel better," Dwylah went on. "We've got a surprise for you."

Dan frowned as he glanced down at her, and then he looked up just as the stranger came out into the hall.

Nick couldn't believe it. Dan was there! He was safe! He was back! Powerful emotions filled him, and he couldn't stop himself as he came forward to his brother.

It was as he took the first step that their gazes met.

Dan went still as he found himself face-to-face with his brother. He would have recognized him anywhere. "Nick—"

"Danny!"

The two men covered the distance between them in a flash and threw their arms around each other in a desperate, emotional reunion.

"It's really you?" Nick choked.

"It's me, Nick. And it's you?" he countered, clasping his brother to him in a tight man hug.

"You'd better believe it—" Nick answered, still not letting him go.

Penny stood back with her father and Dwylah watching their reunion, with tears burning in her eyes. Dan's brother had found him! After all this time, they were together again.

From the parlor doorway, Steve stood with Lacey, beaming with happiness. He tugged on her arm and when she glanced down at him, he told her, "I knew we'd find him."

Lacey bent down and gave the boy a loving hug. "And it's all because of you, Steve. You're the reason they're back together again."

Steve swelled with heartfelt emotion at her words. "I'm glad."

Lacey lifted her gaze to the two brothers and said, "So am I."

Dan and Nick finally moved apart to look at each other in amazement.

"How did you find me?" Dan asked.

"You aren't going to believe it," Nick began.

"Try me."

"Well," Nick said, holding out a hand to Steve.

Steve ran to take it and looked up at the reverend's brother. "Hi, Danny! I'm Steve."

"It's nice to meet you, Steve," Dan replied, a little confused.

"If I hadn't run away from the orphanage, Reverend Miller wouldn't have seen you getting on the train!" Steve smiled triumphantly up at him.

Dan had assumed Steve was Nick's son and the woman standing in the back was his wife, but he knew now he was wrong. "I need to hear this story. I think it's going to be real interesting."

Jack spoke up. "Let's go in the parlor." His reunion with Penny had been wonderful, but he knew seeing the two brothers reunited again after all this time was just amazing.

"We've got a lot of catching up to do," Dan said.

Nick started to move ahead of him with Steve to join Lacey, while Dan waited for Penny to join him.

Penny was so excited, she went to him and pulled him down for a quick kiss. "I am so happy for you—"

Jack looked over at them just then and was surprised by their embrace. "Is there something going on here I don't know about?" he growled.

Penny and Dan looked over at him and they both smiled.

Dan decided to set things straight right then. "We were all set to tell you, but then finding Nick here . . . Well, Jack, I'd like your permission to marry your daughter."

Jack looked between the two of them. "And what does she have to say about this?"

"I already told him yes, Papa, but he insisted on doing this the proper way."

"I knew he was a good man." He turned and looked at Dan. "Yes, you may marry my daughter."

"Thank you, Jack." Dan was serious as he extended his hand to shake hands with his future father-in-law.

The older man took it, thrilled to know Dan was going to be family. He couldn't have chosen any better if he'd arranged it himself.

Dwylah spoke up, having watched everything that had transpired with delight. "So you're getting married?"

"That's right," Dan said, "and it's all thanks to you."

"Me?"

"You're the best chaperone ever," Dan told her, and this time he went to her and kissed her on the cheek.

Dwylah actually blushed. "Oh, Danny, you are a sweet one. She is one lucky girl."

"Yes, I am," Penny agreed.

And they all went into the parlor, where Nick and the others were waiting for them.

"Congratulations," Nick wished them as they all settled in.

"Thank you," Dan and Penny responded.

As they began to talk, Dwylah noticed that Lacey seemed quite distant, sitting back away from everyone as she was. She got up and went to her.

"Want to help me make some tea and coffee?" she invited.

"I'd love to." Lacey was feeling quite out of place and was glad for the chance to slip away with Dwylah.

When they were in the kitchen, Dwylah asked, "How long have you known Nick and Steve?"

"Not long," she hedged.

"Steve said something about you being on the stagecoach with them coming to Sagebrush."

Lacey knew there was no point in trying to hide anything. "Yes, I was anxious to get to Sagebrush and get a new job."

"So, did you get hired while you were in town?" Going with her instincts, Dwylah knew there was more to her story than what she was revealing.

"No. Everywhere I checked I was turned down."

"What can you do?"

"I'm willing to try just about anything—within reason."

Dwylah understood and admired her. She

could tell she was a strong, smart young woman. "So, what do you think of Steve and the reverend? It's seems that little boy is quite taken with you."

"Oh, I adore him. He is such a special boy. I was thinking the other day that if I had some way to support myself I'd adopt him, but—"

"We'll just have to work on finding you a job."

"Thank you, Dwylah."

They finished preparing the hot drinks and carried the tray back into the parlor to find the conversation had turned to the upcoming wedding.

"Since I'm never going to get Danny to the justice of the peace, why don't you marry them?" Dwylah asked the reverend. "Why, you could do it tomorrow! We could have a Christmas wedding. That would be perfect."

Jack looked to his daughter. "What do you think? It's your wedding."

Penny was thrilled, and to know that Dan's long-lost brother was a minister who could marry them just made things even more wonderful. "I'd love to—"

Dan smiled down at her. "So would I."

Nick looked at Dan and Penny, and he could tell how truly in love they were. "I would be honored to perform the ceremony for you."

"It's settled. You'll be married tomorrow," Jack announced.

"We've got some plans to make," Penny said excitedly to Dwylah.

"Let's get started," the older woman agreed eagerly. "This is the best Christmas Eve I've ever had."

Dwylah and Penny headed upstairs to start arranging things for the wedding.

"I didn't bring any fancy gowns with me," Penny told her as they went into her bedroom.

"Don't worry about it. Dan will think you're beautiful no matter what dress you're wearing," Dwylah reassured her. "Let's see what you've got hanging up in here."

Penny opened her wardrobe to show her the few dresses and gowns she'd brought along. Dwylah was thoughtful for a moment and then pulled out a blue gown.

"This color will be perfect on you. Try it on for me."

Penny quickly took off her working clothes, and with Dwylah's help, she donned the blue gown.

"I was right," Dwylah said as she stepped back to study Penny in the dress. The lace-trimmed, square neckline was demure, and the gown was fitted at the waist. Dwylah remembered all too well the full-skirted fashions of years past and the hoops they'd had to wear, and she appreciated the more slim-skirted style that was the fashion these days. "It's simple yet elegant.

It's perfect for your wedding day. You look beautiful."

"I always thought I'd be wearing a white gown," Penny said with a wry smile.

"Do you really care what color your gown is as long as Danny's going to be waiting for you in front of the reverend?" Dwylah asked with a twinkle in her eye.

"Should I just wear my work clothes?" she joked.

"Knowing Danny, he'd married you no matter what you were wearing, you lucky girl!"

"Oh, Dwylah!" Penny gave the older woman a crushing hug. "Thank you so much for coming with me on this trip. I don't know what I would have done without you."

Dwylah hugged her back. "I love you, Penny, dear, and I want you and Danny to live happily ever after."

They hugged for a moment longer and then moved apart as Dwylah grew serious again.

"Now, let's see about what jewelry you're going to wear and decide how we're going to style your hair."

It was getting late, and Jack was exhausted. Lacey had already put Steve to bed and retired for the night. But he wanted a moment to talk privately with his foreman. "Dan, let's go in the study."

Dan looked to his brother. "I'll be right back."

"I'll be waiting for you," Nick said.

Jack closed the door and turned to face him. "I want to know what happened out there. Who shot you?"

"It was John."

"John?" Jack had known the man was stupid, but he'd never thought he was that stupid.

"Evidently he overheard us talking about your money. He ran the horses off and he tried to rob us. I went after him and that's when he shot me."

"What did you do?"

"The fight got ugly then, and he ended up falling off the trail."

"I'm just glad you're all right. Well, I've kept you from your brother long enough. I think he might want to talk to you for a while. And you two help yourself to whatever's in the liquor cabinet. I got the feeling you could use a drink tonight."

"Thanks, Jack."

Dan went back to his brother, while Jack went up to his room.

Dan and Nick stayed on in the parlor. They needed some private time alone to catch up on all they'd missed over the years. Dan went to the liquor cabinet to fix them each a drink.

"So, tell me what happened that night you ran away from the orphanage," Nick said. "Why did you run away?"

"You knew?" Dan was surprised by his question.

Nick nodded. "I ran off from the Millers and came back to be with you."

Dan was shocked. "But you had a new family that wanted you."

Nick met his gaze straight on as he told him, "You were my family, Dan, and you still are."

"What happened when you ran off that way?"

"Miss Helen sent word to the Millers and they came back for me. I kept hoping you'd return to the orphanage while I was there, and I did sneak out at night looking for you, but I couldn't find you anywhere."

Memories of those horrible days and nights when he'd been living on the streets, trying to survive, returned. "I wanted it that way. I thought the orphanage would send someone out to find me, so I made sure I hid real good."

"How did you survive?"

"I took whatever work I could find to feed myself, and gradually I ended up here in Texas. I met Jack and I've been working for him ever since. What about you?"

"I knew after what happened that I had to somehow make things better for orphans who ended up like we did. I never stopped worrying about you, and I didn't want that to happen to any other children. That's why when Steve ran away that day, I had to go find him."

Dan knew the story now and he smiled at his brother. "For all that Steve gave you so much trouble, I'm glad he did. We wouldn't be sitting here together if he hadn't."

"I owe that boy a lot," Nick agreed.

"He seems like he's a good boy."

"He is."

They fell silent for a moment, remembering their own hard times.

"What are you going to do now?" Dan asked. "Do you want to stay here in Sagebrush?"

"I do like it here, but I have to go back. The children need me."

"I'm sure they do." Dan could tell his brother had turned out to be a fine, honorable man. "Way back then, I would never have thought you'd grow up to be a preacher."

"God calls us all to use our gifts in different ways."

They talked long into the night and finally knew they had to get some rest. They gave each other one last brotherly hug and then moved apart.

As Dan started out to his cabin, Nick told him, "Merry Christmas, big brother."

"Merry Christmas, Nick."

"Keep an eye out for Santa while you're out there."

"I will."

"Let's just hope neither one of us gets coal this year."

The two men were smiling as they called it a night.

*   *   *

It was in the wee hours of the morning that Lacey crept out of the small bedroom they'd given her at the far end of the hall. She moved silently down the stairs and into the parlor, where she left Steve's gift on the mantel. She was surprised to find that there were two other packages there with Steve's name on them. Santa had truly come to the Lazy Ace that night.

No one saw or heard her as she returned to her room, and Lacey was glad. She knew this was turning out to be one very special Christmas for everyone. She'd been on her own for so long now that just seeing the two brothers reunited after all this time filled her heart with hope. She knew now that prayers did get answered, but they were answered in God's own time, not man's. Lacey was smiling as she went back to bed.

Chapter Twenty-six

Steve awoke at first light and started to race from the room he was sharing with the reverend, wearing just his nightshirt.

Nick woke up. "Where do you think you're going?"

"It's Christmas!" Steve exclaimed.

Nick started chuckling as he threw off his covers and started to dress. "You're right. Let's get downstairs and see what Santa brought. But first, you need to get dressed. There are ladies staying here, you know."

Steve realized then that he was still in his nightshirt, and he quickly threw it off and pulled on his clothes. They both finished dressing at about the same time and left their bedroom to go downstairs together.

"Nick! Look! Santa did come!" Steve cried out when he saw the gifts on the mantel, and more packages on the floor.

His cries roused the rest of the house, and soon Dwylah, Penny, Lacey, and Jack had joined them in the parlor.

"Merry Christmas!" Jack said. "It looks like Santa found us last night."

"Yes, he did!" Steve's excitement was real.

"Someone better go wake up Dan," Jack said.

"I'll get him," Nick offered. Then he told the boy, "Don't go opening any presents until we get back."

"Yes, sir," Steve said, wanting desperately to rip them open right then, but knowing he had to behave himself.

It took only a few minutes, and the two brothers returned to the house.

The minute Dan came through the door, he looked around for Penny and she came straight to him.

"Merry Christmas," he told her, slipping an arm around her to draw her close.

"Merry Christmas."

They followed the others into the parlor.

As Steve opened his presents, he was thrilled to find that Santa had brought him candy and a book and his very own cowboy hat. He immediately put the hat on and walked proudly around the room, showing it off.

The adults enjoyed watching him and knew the best gift of all was Steve's delight.

Dan had told the ranch hands about the wedding that afternoon, and as the hour drew near they were all eager to come up to the house and watch them get married.

Dwylah had taken charge, moving most of the furniture out of the way so there would be room for everyone. She couldn't wait to see the expression on Danny's face when he got his first look at his bride in her lovely gown. She was thrilled for them both.

Dan was waiting with Nick in the parlor with everyone gathered round. He was wearing his best clothes and he was anxious for the ceremony to begin. The thought that Penny was going to be his bride left him smiling.

"She's coming now." Dwylah hurried in to where they were standing to tell them so they could get ready.

Nick looked at his brother. "You ready for this?"

"Oh yeah."

They turned back to look toward the doorway just as Penny appeared there with her father.

Penny looked into the room to see Dan waiting for her. Her heartbeat quickened at the sight of him, so tall and darkly handsome in his dress clothes. It didn't matter to her that this wasn't the fairy-tale wedding she'd always dreamed of. What mattered was that Dan loved her and she loved him, and they were going to be together forever.

"Now, Penny?" Jack asked as he took her arm.

"Yes, Papa," she told him softly, and she kissed his cheek.

Jack escorted her to Dan's side. He handed her over to Dan and stepped away.

Penny gazed up at Dan and knew this was the happiest day of her life.

Dan stared down at his bride, entranced by her beauty. She'd fashioned her hair in an upswept style and the pale blue gown she was wearing was elegant.

"Dearly beloved, we are gathered here today to join this couple in holy matrimony," Nick began.

Looking at the young couple, Dwylah beamed as the ceremony continued.

"Do you, Dan Roland, take this woman, Penelope Anderson, to be your lawfully wedded wife—for better or worse, for richer or poorer, in sickness and in health until death do you part?" Nick intoned.

"I do," Dan answered.

"And do you, Penelope Anderson, take this man, Dan Roland, to be your lawfully wedded husband—for better or worse, for richer or poorer, in sickness and in health until death do you part?"

"I do."

"I now pronounce you man and wife," Nick proclaimed. He turned to his brother. "You may kiss your bride."

Dan didn't need any encouragement. He gathered Penny into his arms and kissed her, just as all the ranch hands started hollering their congratulations.

Jack came up to them first to kiss his daughter and to shake hands with his new son-in-law. "Welcome to the family, Dan."

"Thanks, Jack."

Dwylah sought out the reverend. "So, what are your plans now? Are you going to stay on for a while?"

"Steve and I will stay on for another week. It's such a blessing that everything turned out so well. I still can't believe that I've really found my brother."

"You're very fortunate. Some families are lost forever."

"I know."

"Have you talked to Lacey about possibly going to work at the orphanage with you? She strikes me as someone who's not afraid of hard work, and she's proven herself to be so good with Steve."

Nick hadn't considered the idea, but now that Dwylah had suggested it, he found it was a good one.

"And," she added with a twinkle in her eye, "if Lacey does decide to go back to the city with you, I can be your chaperone for the trip. I did a fine job bringing Penny out here with Dan. I could do the same for you." She winked. She had a feeling Nick and Lacey would make wonderful, loving parents for little Steve.

"I'll speak with her about it," he told her.

"Good. You do that." Dwylah was grinning as she moved away.

Jack had arranged for the cook to fix them a big dinner, and they enjoyed the meal, celebrating the wedding and Christmas.

Penny liked dining with everyone, but she kept glancing toward Dan, wanting to slip away with him for their wedding night.

"This is a good meal, but I liked the celebration dinner you fixed up at the line shack better," Dan told her in a low voice.

She smiled, remembering their night at the shack. "So did I."

Dan finally decided it was time for them to make their escape. "Are you ready to go, Mrs. Roland?"

"Yes, are you?"

He nodded and they got up to leave the table. "My wife and I are going to leave now."

Everyone was laughing and smiling as they put on their coats and left the house for his small cabin. Dan didn't hesitate. As dressed up as she was, the minute they started from the porch, he swept her up in his arms to carry her.

"Oh, Dan, what about your arm?" Penny worried.

"It's fine. Give me a kiss, woman."

She obliged quickly as she linked her arms around his neck.

Dan wasted no time carrying her to his cabin, and he paused only long enough to open the door before carrying her over the threshold.

"We're home," he said softly as he kicked the door shut behind them.

"Alone, at last," she sighed as he put her down.

While Dan locked the door and let down the

plain curtains that hung on his one window, Penny slipped out of her coat and looked around. The main room of the cabin was nicely furnished, and she moved on to the back to check out the bedroom.

Dan saw where she was headed, and, after leaving his coat behind, he didn't hesitate to go after her. He came up behind her and slipped his arms around her, pulling her back against him as he pressed a kiss to the side of her neck. "You are one beautiful woman, Penny."

"Do you really think so?" A shiver of excitement trembled through her.

He turned her in his arms and answered her with a searing kiss that ignited the fire of her own desire. Dan felt her response and reached behind her to unfasten her gown. It didn't take him long to free her of the garment and it slipped away from her to lie on the floor around her. She was clad only in her undergarments as he lifted her up in his arms again to carry her to his bed. He put her down on the bed and then joined her there.

Penny looked up at him and smiled. "I like this bed much better than the bottom bunk at the line shack."

"So do I," he said with a grin. He wondered for a moment if she was going to ask him if he wanted to be on the top or on the bottom, before he kissed her again.

Penny responded fully to his magical kisses

and surrendered to his lovemaking with innocence and excitement. They came together then,
one in mind and body, as they celebrated the joy
of their vows. They were man and wife.

A long time later, as they lay together, savoring
the wonder of their loving, Penny rolled to her
side and smiled at her husband.

"I got the best Christmas present ever," she told
him softly as she reached out to caress his chest.
"I got a cowboy for Christmas."

Dan smiled as he drew her to him for another
passionate kiss. He knew they were going to live
happily ever after.

Epilogue

Dear Aunt Matilda,

Thank you for your condolences on Papa's death last month. It was a sad time for all of us, but I'm so thankful I got to spend these last months with him. I loved him very much.

Things here at the ranch are going well. Dan and I are very happy, and with the baby coming this fall, life is going to be even more exciting.

Thanks for the news about Amanda and Richard's wedding. Unfortunately, with the baby on the way, Dr. Clemens didn't think it would be wise for me to make such a long trip.

We'd love to have you come visit us for Thanksgiving. Nick and Lacey are going to be here with Steve, and Dwylah tells us there may be wedding bells in their future! Dwylah's been staying in touch with Lou, one of our ranch hands, so why don't you come and bring her with you? We'd certainly have fun, and it would be good to see you. Look forward to hearing from you.

Love,
Penny and Dan

INTERACT WITH DORCHESTER ONLINE!

Want to learn more about your favorite books and authors?
Want to talk with other readers that like to read the same books as you?
Want to see up-to-the-minute Dorchester news?

VISIT DORCHESTER AT:
DorchesterPub.com
Twitter.com/DorchesterPub
Facebook.com (Search Pages)

DISCUSS DORCHESTER'S NOVELS AT:
Dorchester Forums at DorchesterPub.com
GoodReads.com
LibraryThing.com
Myspace.com/books
Shelfari.com
WeRead.com